THI

MW00616949

The Wrong Brother

Copyright: Revised Edition February, 2015
Cover Design: The Killion Group, Inc.
Nancy Brophy
ISBN: 978-0-9862354-2-9

Contact Nancy at: www.NancyBrophy.com
NancyBrophy@gmail.com

The Wrong Series

Each SEAL team member has a core belief that has led him to become the best of the best. No one becomes a SEAL for public adoration. It doesn't happen, at least not on an individual level. The work to make the team is almost impossible. Only a very few achieve it. The decision to leave is gut wrenching. If one chooses not the make the Navy a lifetime commitment, then who is he? Who will he become? Will he ever achieve this same satisfaction, beyond being an adrenaline junkie, in another career?

This series is about men who are ex-SEALs or in the case Zack Pritchard on their way out. They are stories of men who struggle to transfer their beliefs, values and training into careers as private civilians while retaining the same sense of dedication and honor.

Book 1 – The Wrong Brother
Zack and Chloe

This is what lying got you – the wrong brother.

Book 2 – The Wrong Hero
Travis and Abby

"If this is a chess game, then the one thing you should have been able to predict is that the queen always protects the king.

Book 3 – The Wrong Cop
Grant and Dori

"It pisses me off I'm attracted to you." He glared.
"Well, stop it then."
He sneered. "Great advice. How's that working for you?"
"You're like the wad of gum on the sole of my shoe. Only worth as much consideration as it takes to get rid of you."

Book 3.5 - Bonus book –
The Wrong Lover
Marshall and Lily

Her brown eyes and raspy voice stayed with him. Her taste lingered on his lips. After this fiasco was over,

*he'd find her. All he knew was that her name was
Lily, but it wasn't her name he was after.*

This book is dedicated to the Hooligans without whom I would have never been published. Thanks to Linda Kaye, Susan Lute, Darla Luke, Jessica Smith, Linda Smith, Cassiel Knight,

THE WRONG
BROTHER

Nancy Brophy

Chapter One

Zack Pritchard parked the innocuous four-door gray rental on the side street around the corner from his mother's home. Without forethought he expertly wedged the vehicle between two other equally bland cars beneath a shady tree.

He lifted his duffle from the trunk, scanning the empty street as standard routine. Paying attention to details had saved his life more than once.

Bushes, clustered against the white clapboard home on the corner lot, shuddered. His focus sharpened at the same time his muscles tensed. Fingers uncurled from the luggage strap, silently he unzipped a pocket and wiggled his hand inside until the cool steel of his gun was within his grasp. His legs separated into a fighting stance, bending at the knee. Low to the ground, the leaves trembled. He crouched.

A calico cat with two matching kittens pranced out and proceeded haughtily across the lawn, ignoring Zack, even when he burst out laughing. The sound startled him. It'd had been a while since he'd found joy in life.

Habits were hard to break. His hometown, Riggers, Texas was not under a terrorist threat. And his sweet younger sister Glyn's marriage was hardly a covert op. Nor was his arrival a surprise. He glanced at his watch. Other than the fact he was an hour early.

He hoped the cat wasn't an omen. Was he going to jump and twitch at every noise or sudden movement? That'd make for some attractive wedding photos.

Being alert made sense even on leave, but he

needed to dial it back a notch. The paved alley was lined with tall fences and square plastic trashcans. Three houses in, he entered his mother's yard through the wooden back gate.

No cars were parked in the driveway. More than likely no one was home.

Only a flashy, sunshine yellow Ferrari F430 sat on the street as incongruous as mayo on a hot dog. What was a high-powered precision machine doing in a middle class neighborhood in a no-where town in north Texas? Riggers as the name implied, was an oil-boom town. Even if someone had sunk a well and had money to burn, why was a racing machine here?

Before choosing a parking location, Zack had circled the block twice. The second time served no purpose other than to give him another chance to ogle the powerful vehicle. Racing was no longer his life, but rarely did the impetuous days of his youth enter his thinking, so his desire caught him off-guard.

NASCAR. Two years of his life were spent riding the circuit as a backup driver, the bench warmer. Without warning, he joined the Navy. A smile curved his lips as he remembered his drunken stupor, combined with the frustration and rage of an arrogant twenty-year old.

Despite the predicted gloom and doom, his decision was the best thing that ever happened to him. The Navy led him to the SEALs where his life achieved true purpose.

A deep sigh escaped his lips. Would he ever find that raw bone-deep satisfaction again? Or would sitting on the sidelines, watching others do the job he loved, be enough? He hadn't liked being a bench warmer at twenty, somehow he doubted it would have more appeal now. At thirty-three he had reached the upper limit for active SEALs in the field. The Navy liked him, but with each promotion, the thing he loved most was drifting further and further from his grasp.

He wasn't alone. Men on his team who had been with him from the beginning faced the same dilemma. Being a SEAL was a young man's game and everyone knew it, but knowing something and believing it, he'd discovered were two different things. Some of life's lessons were a bitch.

He walked past the detached garage located at the rear of the lot. Dry rot on the window ledges caught his eye. He made a mental note to mention it to his mother.

Down the long driveway, he caught another glimpse of the Ferrari. It belonged to no one he knew unless Glyn had dumped Stan-the-man and snagged a tycoon.

He snorted.

No, if Glyn found a man with money his mother would have published it in every paper in America. Stanley, aka Mr. Safety Goggles, as his younger brother Gordy aptly nicknamed him, lived a risk free, and in Zack's opinion, very boring life. Partly due to his career choice as an OSHA inspector for one of the industrial plants out on the highway and partly because of his personality.

Gordy should be the one getting married. He'd dated Chloe since high school. The first time Zack met her, she'd bounced like a cheerleader and her stick-thin gangly body sported the grace of a newborn giraffe. But any awkwardness had been overcome with the adorable smile and golden brown puppy-dog eyes that dominated her face. Perfect for Gordy or so he'd always believed.

Until her grandmother's funeral two years ago.

On his last trip to Texas he'd attended the funeral, expecting to see the same cute kid. Boy, had she knocked the wind out of him. She'd grown up. Smoothed out. Still slender and willowy, but with soft curves that called to a man. And breasts, the perfect size to fill a man's hands. Her heart shaped face still hosted big brown eyes but the rest of her features had caught up with them. Particularly that mouth. Oh, man, the things he could do with those perfect shiny lips.

Chloe La Ruse.

Zack would never have admitted it publicly. But Chloe had been the object of some pretty incredible fantasies. Holed up in tight situations in foreign countries with unpronounceable names, he'd found concentrating on the pretty blonde with the velvety golden skin kept him from losing his mind. She reminded him of autumn, all shades of rich gold and warm brown tones with flashes of heat-filled oranges and reds.

He hadn't seen her in person since that day, but the effect on his body hadn't lessened. He never imagined she'd cling in his mind like a burr he couldn't shake.

If it'd had just been the funeral he'd have been okay, but his mother, after ignoring Chloe to the point of rudeness, reversed herself and insisted she join them for dinner.

Following the meal, the rest of his family disappeared, leaving Zack and Chloe alone. At her suggestion they'd moved outside to watch a spectacular sunset in the fading daylight and the sweltering Texas heat. She was the only woman he'd ever known who hated breathing the chemical air manufactured by a forced air cooling as much as he did.

They sat on the steps of the wooden deck. Zack avoided staring at the yellow dress molding her breasts. A line of dewdrops beaded above her delectable lips. Hell, he prayed he wasn't drooling as he struggled to have thoughts that didn't involve kissing his brother's girlfriend.

And where was his brother? Gordy was so enamored he'd gone to play computer games in his room. Alone.

The muted television noise drifted from the family room. "What exactly do you do in the SEALs?"

He answered, but stumbled over his words, losing any hope for smoothness. To cover his behavior he took her hand and touched the delicate skin of her wrist under the pretense of offering her comfort over the funeral. She shivered, but hadn't withdrawn her hand. That signal from any other woman would have encouraged him to charge ahead.

He forced himself to hold back, to not think about her lips or the warm caress of her skin or the way her scent of oranges and wild honeysuckle filled his nostrils. The demons that drove him wanted her. He went so far as to glance around for a dark corner where he could peel away the dress from her body to expose what was underneath.

If she hadn't been Gordy's...

He wouldn't go there this time. The last visit had been tough enough, keeping his hands off her. Gordy didn't deserve her.

And Zack couldn't have her.

He gritted his teeth. This couldn't go any further. If Gordy still dated Chloe, he would ignore her or treat her as a kid sister. Yeah, that was the best solution.

Bolstering his resolve he grabbed the back doorknob. A grimace crossed his face. The door gave without hesitation. His mother had taken no precautions despite Zack's warnings. People in small towns believed themselves to be inviolable, but they weren't. He set his bag on the floor of the mudroom and sank to the bench to unlace his boots.

"Gordy, no." The feminine voice that haunted his dreams protested. "We don't have time." Except the words were different. In his fantasies, she begged, murmuring desperate words in his ear, *"Zack, yes, now."*

"Sure we do," Gordy said. His pleading words were a little slurred, probably from lust. If Chloe had belonged to Zack, he'd keep her naked in his bed until she was too sated to look at any other man but him. He'd recognized Gordy's tone as the same one he used with their mother to get his way.

"My brother won't be here for at least half an hour. That's plenty of time."

Zack considered dropping a boot to announce his presence. Gordy had his own place. Why would he want to have sex in his mother's house? Zack shuddered at the repugnant idea.

"I've got to go to school."

Keep up that defense, honey.

"You never want to do it anymore."

Zack wanted to smack his brother. Could he sound whinier?

Chloe's voice rose in either protest or irritation, Zack couldn't decide which. "That's not true."

"Yeah, it is."

Visualizing Gordy's sulky pout was easy.

"Well, when was the last time you allotted more than fifteen minutes?"

Oh, great. A full-blown argument about sex. Maybe he'd go out and come back in again. He looked at his boots sitting on the floor and sighed. No, he needed to say something like, knock it off.

"You know I'm not into that mushy stuff." Aw, nuts. His brother defended his sloppy behavior. "Besides we had real sex a couple of weeks ago."

A silence followed. Now was his time.

He stepped toward the kitchen only to hear Chloe say, "Do you mean when you got drunk and passed out on top of me? That wasn't a couple of weeks ago, that was before Christmas and if that's your idea of real sex, I don't know why we bother."

Before Christmas? This was May.

And when he looked into two startled eyes the color of warm honey and saw the slow blush creeping up her cheeks, he didn't know why the floor didn't open up and swallow him whole.

"I can't help that I love you, babe." Gordy complained from somewhere deeper in the kitchen.

"Shut up, Gordon." Chloe croaked, her voice barely above a whisper. "Zack's here." Nervously, she touched her pink tongue to her pretty lips. His gaze followed the movement. The sound of a scraping chair changed the direction of his thinking.

"Zack!" Gordy hollered, his desire for Chloe forgotten. "Man, great to see you." His brother bolted forward, bringing with him the stench of sour alcohol, and wrapped his arms around him.

Fourteen hundred hours on a Tuesday and his brother was drunk.

"What happened to you?" Zack asked, reeling from the hug. "You been in fight or something?" He steered his brother to a chair. Gordy had lost weight. His below-the-ears hair had bottled blond streaks running through the light brown. His cheekbones were hollowed out giving him a gaunt look Zack hadn't seen before. The new clothes were stylish. A pressed black t-shirt and slacks covered by a subtle brown and black plaid jacket. In fact if it hadn't been for the alcohol and his battered face, Gordy looked like a male model.

"Nothin' happened to me." Gordy glanced in the mirror as he plopped onto his seat. "You should see the other guy." He grinned at Zack before resting his head on folded arms supported by the table.

Male model or not, Zack spent too much time in bars not to recognize certain signs. In minutes his brother would pass out. Apparently, Chloe knew the signs, as well.

"You have to take me to school. You can't go to sleep now," she said, using a snappy, crisp voice reminiscent of his third grade teacher, Miss Evans.

In response, Gordy made a snarfling noise and closed his eyes.

"Forget it," Zack said. "I'll give you a ride."

His brother wasn't completely gone, because he warbled. "Yeah, he'd give you a ride you'd never forget. Then maybe you'd be worth screwing."

Chloe whirled away before Zack caught her expression, for which he was grateful. How the hell had he gotten in the middle of this fight? Chloe stood at the window staring into the backyard.

What would he do if she cried? He'd have to put his arm around her, that's what. But he'd hold himself in check and not allow the situation to get out of hand.

The boy emitted a loud snore. Zack watched drool run out his swollen open lips. How old was he now? Twenty-six? Zack was embarrassed to say it, but Gordy needed a firm boot to the ass. What the hell was wrong with him?

"I'm parked around the block."

Her head bobbed in lieu of a reply. Skirting around him, she avoided looking his direction as she headed toward the living room. Zack padded out to the mudroom and grabbed his duffle. "Are you in a hurry? Or do I have enough time to grab a shower and change clothes?"

"We don't have to leave for about thirty minutes." Her quiet voice sounded normal, not choked up or anything. Good, the plan was working.

Zack carried the duffle down the hall to the guest bedroom. His mother had painted the walls and replaced the carpet since the last time he'd been home. Beige on beige. Even the drapes lacked color. The house he'd called home for eighteen years no longer held any life.

His bedroom was located at the front of the house. He pushed open the door to see clothes scattered randomly across the bed. Four or five feminine shoes in search of mates randomly dotted the floor. Soft canvas suitcases were tumbled into a corner.

"You're upstairs. Your cousin, Valerie wanted

this room." Chloe said, not two feet behind him.

"Upstairs?" He avoided her eyes. But with her standing so close his other option was to stare at her chest. She wasn't helping things. Her direct gaze, neither shy nor retiring, challenged him in unexpected ways.

"In Gordon's old room. Valerie's son, Aiden, is also staying in there."

"It's only got a single bed."

A grin flitted across her face. "And an air mattress set up for you."

"Forget it. I'll stay at a motel." He grabbed the duffle and hoisted it over his shoulder. He would have kept moving, but she blocked the door and didn't appear in any hurry to move.

"I offered to let you stay in my second bedroom, but your mother vetoed the idea. She thought you'd be uncomfortable."

She thought right. No way could he stay at her place. "Of course not. I wouldn't want to put you out."

"Oh, your mother wasn't worried that you'd stand on ceremony. She thought the biggest problem was the fact you don't like me."

Yeah, that could be a problem, if only it were true.

Zack had the feeling he was caught between two unseen forces. He swallowed hard. He was a man, damn it. Not a saint. Not a hero. There was only so much temptation he could resist.

Staying at Chloe's would be like sending a match to a tinder festival. This was the worst idea ever. He swallowed again. His throat had never been so dry.

Chloe appeared to know he liked her fine. In fact she seemed to be taunting him but he couldn't be one hundred percent sure that wasn't wishful thinking on his part.

"She's wrong. I don't dislike you. If you've got room, I'm more than willing to stay at your place."

Brave talk for a man who swore he wasn't going to sleep with his brother's girlfriend.

Hell, he was turning out to be as big a schmuck as Gordy. Both of them deserved to have their asses kicked.

Chapter Two

Chloe followed Zack out to the car. What had she done? Leaped into the fire. And why? Because Bernice hated her and Chloe wanted to prove her wrong.

Her apartment was small. Tiny even. At night she'd be able to hear him breathe. Could she sleep, knowing he was in the next room, breathing in and out all night long? Where was her brain? Even as she chastised herself, she watched his butt flex with each step he took. The man had a way of filling out a pair of jeans. The black t-shirt did nothing to hide his powerful chest and muscular arms.

Gordy never affected her like this. It had been years since Gordy affected her at all. After Gram's funeral they'd broken up. But every couple of months or so he still came around. She hadn't objected. It wasn't like she was seeing anyone else.

There were nights when it had been comforting to have him with her when all he wanted was to snuggle and talk. He still made the obligatory offer, but that was all ego. He wasn't interested in having sex any more than she was.

Despite those problems she'd breathed a sigh of relief when he'd agreed to go to tomorrow's class. At the end of the summer, she'd leave for Indiana and a new group of people. It'd be a while before others realized something was inherently wrong with her. Men weren't attracted to her for anything other than sex. Gordy was the only man who'd hung around for any length of time. And wasn't that sad? Men who wanted something more than a quick fling avoided tongue-tied women who fell over their own feet.

"Where to?" Zack asked as they approached the street.

"My apartment's adjacent to the campus. I can walk to class from there."

He glanced at his watch as he held the door open for her. "What time's your class?"

"Three o'clock." Chloe forced herself to take calming deep breaths so that by the time he walked around the car and was seated inside, she could carry on a decent conversation.

I am at one with the Universe.

Zack slid onto the seat, snapped his belt in place and cranked the key. "What're you taking?"

Good. School. A topic she could talk about without fumbling. "Nothing. I'm finishing my thesis this semester and teaching a couple of intro courses."

"You're in graduate school?"

He sounded impressed. Not for long, if he shared his brother's narrow views about school and her major. Her temper flashed. She didn't even know why she'd invited him to stay. It was going to be one long week. Zack had been so nice to her after Gram's funeral, but then his brother could be nice, too. He probably wouldn't turn out to be any different from Gordy.

No negative thinking. I am able, accepting, calm and caring.

Breathing deeply, she answered his question. "Master's program." Chloe regretted his dark aviator glasses made it impossible to read his thoughts. She stared out the passenger window and forced herself to still her hands, crossed, then uncrossed her legs. Get it over with. Just tell him. It can't get any worse.

Twisting in the seat she faced him. The smile and raised eyebrows she sported gave him the opportunity to regard it as a joke.

"Introductiontohumansexuality." There was nothing he could say, she hadn't already heard.

She had to give him credit. His face remained unchanged. He didn't grin. He didn't smirk. He didn't even raise an eyebrow.

"So what's today's topic?" he asked as though he carried on an intellectual conversation about sex every day of the week.

"Erectile dysfunction." She tilted her head, waiting for his reaction. Gordy would have groaned and acted repulsed. Zack said nothing as he signaled to make the left hand turn onto the street in front of the University.

"Based upon the conversation I overheard, it sounds like you're well versed in that arena."

This was so not happening. Discussing her sex problems with her ex-boyfriend's brother was not possible. But she'd opened this can of worms. How to steer him in a different direction? "How long are you staying?"

"A week, maybe less."

Her breathing came a little easier. "Gordon tells me you work with a team in the Navy. What are they doing while you're gone?"

"Overseas assignment, known as OCONUS. Out of the continental United States."

"You're skipping that? I'll bet you're disappointed."

He laughed and she had the feeling she'd missed a private joke.

"They're not on vacation. It's a training exercise," he said. "Tell me where to turn."

Maybe she'd do a little research on Navy SEALs at the computer this evening or maybe not, if he was going to be there. She pointed. He drove into the parking lot of her four-plex and parked in the only empty spot between her powder blue Pinto and the neighbor's pickup.

"Talk about a death trap," Zack hoisted his duffle out of the trunk while staring at the car in the next spot. "I didn't even know those cars existed anymore."

"It's a classic." Could she sound more defensive?

Zack turned his head at her words. "It's yours?" His look of startled surprise said everything. She nodded, unable to think of words to justify her choice of vehicle.

"How's it run?"

Nice recovery, she had to give him that. Better actually than anything she would have blurted out. "Not at all. It's been sitting there since before Christmas."

"What's wrong?"

She shrugged. "Something that costs money."

Zack followed her up the stairs. The building was solid, brick construction, but fraying at the edges, like so many things in her life. Her furniture had come from Gram's house so she didn't feel so alone. Looking at it with fresh eyes, she could see how Zack might be repelled at the worn, out-of-date chintz covered furniture and the hook rugs.

Then she remembered her workroom. Hurrying across the room, she flung open the door to the second bedroom. The bed was covered with books. Research books. If he hadn't thought anything before, he would now. How many normal people had this many books on sex?

"Give me a minute to clean this up," she said, bustling around the bed.

"Leave it. I've got nothing else to do, I'll get it."

Heat burned her cheeks, no doubt leaving them bright red. Why was it, she could stand before an entire room of freshman and talk about sex for two hours without blushing? But two minutes around the hunky Zack and she fumbled like a novice.

Snap out of it.

Zack stared. "How're you going to teach sex ed if you're embarrassed to be in the same room with sex books?"

"Normally, I'm not, but you're Gordy's brother."

He leaned against the door jamb and folded his arms, his brows knitted together. "From your standpoint, I don't think that's an impressive qualification."

Chloe couldn't have this conversation with Zack. He wouldn't understand her worries. Like all the Pritchard's he'd take Gordy's side, no matter what she said.

"Gordy's all right. When he's not drinking, he's fun. We've been having some problems but everybody does."

Zack crossed the room to gather the books. Chloe bent over to help him.

"Go on," he said. "I'll get it."

Flummoxed, she stopped fussing. "All right." She grabbed her book bag and headed toward the door. Her plan to prove Bernice wrong had backfired big time. Would he even be here when she returned?

Chapter Three

Zack kissed his mother's cheek and handed her the bouquet of colorful flowers. Five-year-old Aidan burst through the kitchen door, completely naked. Aiden's mother, Valerie chased after him, close on his heels.

"No bath," the child yelled, a mischievous grin of delight across his face.

"I brought a new tub toy for you," Valerie bribed as she sprinted past. "Hi."

"Hi, yourself." He said to the back of her head.

"No bath," Aiden squirted through the swinging door into the dining room.

From the dining room, his sister, Glyn hollered, "Gotcha." Valerie slowed to a walk, knowing the slippery five year old was cornered.

A few minutes later, Glyn popped into the kitchen, "That kid's got a future as a track-- Zack, you're here." She threw herself into his arms. "I've been so worried you wouldn't be able to come."

"And miss walking you down the aisle? No way."

"I'm so sorry I can't stay, but I'm meeting Stanley and his parents for dinner. He hates it when I'm late. His father eats on a regular schedule. The MS, you know."

Stanley lived at home, caring for his aging parents with no plans to move when he married. Glyn, being a nurse, probably found that appealing. Stanley, being tight-assed probably saw financial gain in marrying a live-in nurse.

They'd dated for three years. Maybe it'd taken

him that long to map out their life on a spread sheet and decide he could pop the question. To Zack prison would have been more fun.

"You're never on time." He teased her as he had when she was young.

"Of course," Glyn laughed and tossed her head. "The man I marry needs something to worry about."

"Are you hungry?" Without waiting for an answer, his mother opened the refrigerator and pulled out clear plastic storage containers with blue lids. Glyn kissed his cheek and disappeared out the backdoor.

"I'm fine. I ate earlier," he said. "Can you sit for a minute and talk?" He didn't mention the spaghetti he'd made for Chloe and left in her refrigerator.

His mother didn't sit. Instead she piled more plastic containers on the table. Even relaxing at home, his mother projected perfection. Pressed navy slacks, a tidy white blouse and hair perfectly groomed. Maybe that was where Gordy was picking up his fashion sense.

"I can't believe you're not staying here," she said. "When you go to Gordy's tonight, take these with you. I worry he's not eating right."

"You'll have a house full of company and hundreds of things to do before Friday. I'll be in the way." He vetoed telling her Gordy hadn't asked him to stay, Chloe had.

"I suppose it'd be more fun to stay with Gordy anyway. You two can hang out together like the old days."

What old days?

He'd left home right after high school graduation. His brother was seven years younger. After dad died his junior year, he'd spent time with

Glynnis who needed him. He'd nicknamed Gordy, Wolf-boy, because he was never without his pack of buddies.

His mother grabbed a paper bag and stacked plastic containers inside. "Gordy works so hard. He's never at home. This afternoon he fell asleep at this table."

Zack debated telling his mother the truth about Gordy's nap, but before he could say anything, she was onto another subject. "Did he show you his new car? It's so flashy."

"A new car?"

His mother moved to the sink and loaded the dishes into the dishwasher. "A bright yellow Ferrari."

"He can afford a Ferrari?"

"He has a good job. As a salesman. At first I was angry at Chloe for making him drop out of school, but he's done okay and except for that little problem last fall, I'm very proud of him."

Zack sighed, "What little problem last fall?" His mother's gift for understatement could mean any number of things, combined with his skepticism of how a twenty-six-year old could afford that car.

"He got arrested, but it was all Chloe's fault."

"For what?"

Bernice sprinkled cleanser in the kitchen sink. Her next words were obscured by the noise of the running water.

"I didn't hear you."

"Drugs. But they weren't his. He was just holding them for Chloe."

Zack wanted to laugh. His mother was delusional. Her son was a college dropout driving a

Ferrari and had an arrest record. But the problem was his girlfriend who lived in a seedy apartment, drove a POS beater and was finishing grad school. He'd seen her apartment. Not only were books on the bed. They were crammed more packages of Raman Noodles than he'd ever seen outside a grocery store. He'd shopped for ingredients to make spaghetti.

"Gordy's exhausted from hard work. It's what killed your father you know." His mother would never change. She saw only what she wanted and ignored the rest.

"Did you notice Gordy's face?" he asked, wanting to hear her version of the events.

"Awful, wasn't it? Apparently they were in a car accident, just yesterday. Chloe was at the wheel."

"In the Ferrari?"

Bernice sniffed. "Of course not. He'd never let her drive the Ferrari. She's too unreliable. They were in that little blue car, she owns. After Gordy spent all that money getting it fixed."

The Pinto was a beater, but it wasn't a wrecked beater. And those marks on Gordy's face hadn't come from any car accident. Would his mother believe absolutely anything her youngest son told her?

"If she's such a bad influence, why don't they break up?"

"I've encouraged him to, but he's just like his father. So loyal. He can't leave her when she's got problems. Your father was the most courageous man I've ever known…"

Zack tuned his mother out as she drifted down memory lane. He'd heard all the stories, which had gotten considerably better since his father's death. His father had been a short wiry accountant, who'd come home every evening and seldom raised his voice.

Gordy and Glynnis both looked like him. Zack could never figure out how he got into this family. Compared to them, he was a dark-haired giant in the land of short beige people. Six inches taller than Gordy, Zack outweighed him by sixty pounds of solid muscle. Thanks to the Navy.

But his mother couldn't be entirely wrong. He'd watch Chloe a little closer while staying there. If she were as innocent as she appeared, why was she still hanging with his brother? Surely by now they would've broken up. Even this afternoon, she'd said Gordy was fun. What kind of fun were they having?

The phone rang. His mother stopped cleaning long enough to answer. "He's right here," she said, handing him the receiver. "It's your brother."

"Gordy?" Zack asked into the receiver. Music blared in the background.

"Hey, man. Sorry about this afternoon. Are you bored with that hen party at Ma's house yet? C'mon down to the B&L. Have a drink with me."

Seven-forty five. He didn't want to be too late getting back to Chloe's. But one drink, shouldn't take more than an hour or so. And maybe he could get to the bottom of this mess with Chloe and Gordy.

Chapter Four

The B&L was a bar that could have existed in any city in the world. Zack had been in a hundred identical dives. The dark, dank closed smell of whiskey and stale cigarettes was universal, as were the busty waitresses and road-weary bartenders.

Gordy bent over one of the four pool tables in the rear. Early yet, the bar wasn't nearly as full as it would be in another couple of hours.

Zack ordered a beer before he headed back to the poolroom. From his position he had a clear view of the entire place and occupants, including the guy who approached his brother. Biker-looking dude. Scruffy. Long unkempt hair and scraggly beard. Leather vest with chains. Was he the one who'd beaten Gordy?

His brother didn't appear worried. The men touched knuckles and spoke for a minute. Then both abruptly turned to face the back wall; standing so close they almost touched. Zack groaned, knowing that money and baggies were being exchanged.

No wonder Gordy had been busted. Hell, Zack could see a dope deal going down from the far side of the room. Where was Gordy's sense? If Zack didn't get him straightened out on this trip, he would be visiting his brother in Huntsville Prison.

No one paid any attention to the transaction in the poolroom except the biker dude's emaciated girlfriend who slouched in a booth. Even her interest level was minimal.

Grabbing the bottle of beer from the bartender, he ignored the glass and threw down a five. "Keep it." The bartender slid the bill into his pants never ringing up the sale.

"Hey, man," Gordy said as Zack approached. "Grab a stick."

Dolly Parton's sleazy younger sister sidled up to Gordy. "What can I get ya, Sug?" The empty tray at her shoulder swayed in tempo with her hips, both moving to the fast-paced beat of the country and western song blaring from the jukebox.

"Whiskey. Dixie, this here's my brother. Get him anything he wants on my tab."

"Hi, ya. What'da want?" She smacked her gum, thrust an ample hip forward and boldly eyed him up and down.

"I'm set, thanks." Zack gestured to show his beer before studying the selection of pool cues on the paneled wall.

"I'm off at one tonight." She said to Gordy in a stage whisper Zack could plainly hear. "Should I come by?"

"Don't know yet. Check back in an hour," his brother mumbled.

In the Navy, Zack had seen a lot of men make fools of themselves over the wrong women. Witnessing his brother pat the waitress's abundant ass in a familiar gesture reminded him that no one was immune. But Dixie was the least of Gordy's problems.

"Okey dokey." She smacked her gum another time before heading for the bar.

As the waitress sauntered off Gordy racked the table. "Eight ball?"

"Sure."

"You break."

Zack didn't care about the game, but he bent over

the table and stroked the cue stick. Balls ran everywhere.

"You're stripes," Gordy grabbed a square of chalk.

He lined up his second shot. "How come you're not seeing Chloe tonight?"

"You're kidding, right?" His brother snorted. "Ms. Party Pooper will be asleep by nine-thirty."

He was careful not to run the table. The next shot he deliberately missed. "Why are you still with her?"

"Who? Chloe?" As Gordy took his shot, his face caught the light. Bloodshot eyes. The white ball bounced off the bumper before sinking into a pocket. His brother was trashed. Functional, but wasted.

"Yeah."

"What? You think I could take ol' Dixie home to ma's?" he chuckled, as though Zack was a stand-up comedian in his down time. "Plus Dixie's hot. She's not a nut job like Chloe all twisted up with the sex thing."

Zack's cue jerked, causing him to miss. *Chloe was twisted up about sex?* "In what way?"

"She wants to be a therapist - a SEX therapist -- whatever the hell, that is. When I'm doing her, about three times a year anymore, I feel like a freakin' lab rat." Gordy groused. "Hell, she probably takes notes as soon as I fall asleep." He pulled himself together and ran a series of successful shots.

Three times a year? No wonder she chose sex therapy for a career. He wasn't a hound dog, but he had sex a helluva lot more than three times a year. He probed a little deeper. "Mom doesn't like her."

"I know. Great, huh?" He grinned like the eleven-year old imp, he'd been. "No matter what happens, I'm off the hook."

"Maybe with mom," Zack shook his head, trying to sort out how to approach Gordy. One shot followed another as he concentrated on how to break through to his brother. "I heard about the drug bust. Cops aren't so easily fooled." He pointed to the corner pocket indicating his last shot.

Gordy shrugged, unbothered by the potential of a jail sentence. "Yeah, I sold to an undercover cop. Not my best moment, but it's all getting worked out." He scratched his balls and readjusted his jeans.

"How?"

"Got a lawyer who'll get me off."

"I hope so." *This was worse than he thought.* "What'd Chloe say?"

Gordy hawked up a loogie and spit into a spittoon against the wall. "When did you get old and soft? Chloe doesn't know."

Zack looked at his brother long and hard as he bent over the pool table. Riggers had always been a safe haven where his family was quietly tucked away. Glynnis was a nurse marrying a boring guy, but Stanley was safe. Gordy was too dysfunctional to hear him now, but tomorrow they'd get together and have a chat. As a SEAL Zack had a level of responsibility that didn't ignore illegal drug transactions happening in front of him or a brother spinning out of control.

Thirty minutes later, they walked to the car. Gordy stumbled down the stairs, but managed to remain upright. "You don't have to go. Stay. Shoot the shit some more."

Zack shook his head, knowing that if Gordy continued drinking, which he fully expected, in thirty minutes he would be comatose. "Let's get you home." He stretched out a hand to take his brother's arm.

Gordy jerked away. "You kidding? It's early, yet. I'm not going home."

"You're wasted."

Gordy huffed out a laugh. "This ain't nothin'. If you force me to leave, I'll call a ride and be back here in half an hour."

Zack dug in his jeans pocket for his car keys. He hadn't told anybody where he was bunking. Now was the time. It'd be interesting to see how possessive his brother reacted and if all his bluster about his longtime girlfriend was just that. "It's your life. I'm staying at Chloe's and I don't want to get in too late."

A puzzled frown settled on Gordy's features. "She won't know."

What was wrong with him? Didn't he see how appealing she was? He unlocked the car and opened the rear door. "Mom sent you food," and thrust the brown paper bag toward him.

Gordy grimaced and held the bag away from him like it contained smelly diapers. "What're you doing tomorrow?"

"Don't know. Let's get together."

His brother groaned. "Damn. I'd say we could hang out, but I promised Chloe I'd go to some private class with her."

"Private class?"

"These things are brutal. The last one she dragged me to, we watched some old lady jerking her husband off."

"What?"

"It was some sort of technique. Tantric or something like that. Anyway it grossed me out. No way I'd let Chloe practice on me. Jeez. How'd I let her talk me into this again?"

"Why don't you call after it's done?"

"Solid, dude." He held up his scabbed and bruised knuckles to touch Zack's. Another souvenir from his fight.

Zack lowered himself into the driver's seat and watched as his brother walked to the dumpster and tossed his mother's brown sack inside. Who was adopted? Him or Gordy? They couldn't both be from the same parents. Hell, they weren't even from the same planet.

Chapter Five

Chloe stood on the sidewalk, watching for the yellow Ferrari. Damn Gordon. He'd better not have blown her off. She'd been on the waiting list for this class for six months - one on one instruction taught by the infamous sex researcher Marlene Campbell, on the positions of the Kama Sutra. Not the stylized positions drawn in the book that no one but a contortionist could perform, but practical ones adjusted for the normal human body.

Marlene had plenty of offers from voyeurs or understudies. She refused them all, using only serious participants. To be selected the couple had to be engaged in a long-term intimate relationship.

In preparation she dragged him to a lecture on tantric techniques thinking to ease him into the topic. His negative response stunned her. Who wouldn't want to learn more about sex? Who wouldn't want to have even an ex-girlfriend practice on him?

For that reason she'd chosen not to tell him the details of this class, knowing he'd back out. Had she slipped up somehow? Could he have found out?

She shook her head. He didn't give a rat's ass about what she did. More than likely he forgot. She exhaled in exasperation. This whole thing was a mistake. She admitted the truth. She didn't want to have sex with Gordy ever again, even if her career demanded it.

Her heart crashed hard in her chest. He was her last link to her past. Everyone else had left her. Only the two of them remained and he probably wouldn't care when they were no longer connected.

Inexplicably Zack came to mind. Funny she'd

miss him, too. She still remembered the first time they met. Gordy had taken her home to meet his family because his older brother was in town. Even a green seventeen-year-old virgin could see the difference between the lean boy she dated and the man who shook her hand.

His wide shoulders and hard muscled body would have terrified her, except for the kind deep-brown eyes in his tanned face. Until that very moment, she hadn't realized how appealing short hair could be on a man or how facial lines reflected an interesting life.

"This is the kind of man Gordy will grow up to be." That's when she'd decided he was the one for her.

But it hadn't happened that way. Eight years later Gordy had gotten older, but Zack remained her male role model. Even if he didn't care about her, he was nicer than his brother.

Like the spaghetti last night had been a lifesaver. After dragging home late from the library, she'd expected another meal of Ramen Noodles. But when she'd opened the refrigerator on the off chance that there might be something she'd forgotten, a bowl of cooked pasta and container of sauce had waved a greeting with little hand-written notes telling her how to warm it up. And he used real Italian sausage and a marinara sauce that didn't taste like ketchup.

To thank him she'd lain awake listening for the sound of his arrival. At midnight she'd decided he'd found other sleeping arrangements. Disappointed, she crawled out of bed to deadbolt the door.

But she'd found the apartment was already

secured and she hadn't locked up.

The second bedroom door was closed and she'd opened it to take a peek. The only light filtered in from the hallway, but exposed a lump of covers in bed. Not a sound. Was he asleep? If so, he was the quietest sleeper she'd ever known.

If she'd crept closer, he'd smell warm and sinful. And oh, so tempting. But what if he'd thought her presence indicated she was issuing an invitation? What would he do? He was a guy and probably wouldn't say no, except that he was Gordy's brother who disliked her. She eased the door shut and slunk back into her cold, lonely bed.

Now in the heat of the day she tapped the glass face of her watch and faced another truth. Gordy wasn't coming.

She eyed the long sidewalk that led up the steps to Marlene's door. Six months wasted. Forfeiting the tuition would stretch her restricted budget. With each step she bolstered her flagging spirits with uplifting affirmations.

Everything would work out for the best. It always had. The only thing controllable is one's own attitude.

Chloe rang the doorbell. The stately two-story home gave no indication that anything out-of-the-ordinary took place there. No big flashing neon sign on the lawn stating SEX CLASSES HELD HERE. SIGN UP TODAY.

Rather the red brick with white trim and wooden shutters screamed America, the land of wholesome values, apple pie and classes which would improve your sexual performance or at least expand your boundaries.

In the time she'd waited on the curb, three other couples had entered. Everyone was here, but her.

And, of course, Gordon.

While the house may have screamed normal, the woman who answered the door did not. Chloe gaped at the peacock with a face, dressed in swirls of blue and green from head to toe stood before her. Midnight black curls peeked out from the edges of the turban. Silvery blue eyes surrounded by tanned skin, starred at her. Her mouth, a slash of bright red, brightened into a smile.

"Chloe La Ruse," Marlene said in a lilting voice. "Come in. Where's your partner, Gordon Pritchard?"

"Wow, you're good with names." She stalled, allowing one last little flare of hope. "Gordon's late."

"Oh, I'm good with a lot of things." Marlene laughed at her own joke. "But he's not too late. Here he comes now."

Chloe breathed a sigh of relief. Gordy had come through. A grin brightened her face. Karma had ruled in her favor.

"And he was definitely worth waiting for." Pure admiration filled the older woman's voice.

With her smile cemented in place, but with an overwhelming rush of dread Chloe turned toward the street. The man Marlene admired was probably the UPS delivery guy, but she was sure he wasn't Gordy.

Zack was already to the concrete steps when Marlene elbowed Chloe out of the way to hold out her hand in greeting. Shock ran through her body.

Gordy had sent Zack?

Marlene was right. He did look good. "You must be Gordon." It didn't help when Chloe heard a distinct purr in her voice.

He smiled, a lady-killer curl of the lips that had

the woman who was at least twenty years older than him, all but drooling, "I'm sorry I've kept you waiting."

Chloe sucked her bottom lip into her mouth as Marlene raised her hand displaying five blood-red talons and rested it against his chest. "This afternoon is going to be very special."

Okay. She understood the need to touch the muscle-bound man. She felt that way herself. But Zack wasn't hers and he sure as hell wasn't Marlene's.

"I hope so." Zack and Marlene shared a laugh, making Chloe want to beat her head against the brick wall.

This is what lying got you -- the wrong brother.

Why hadn't she just told Gordy the truth? At least he wouldn't have sent his brother in his place -- knowing that physical intimacy would be required. Well, after the crack he made yesterday, he might. Men were so hard to figure out. But right now she had to get Zack out of here.

If she blurted out the truth, Marlene wouldn't care, but she'd probably persuade him to stay. And if Chloe couldn't have him, neither could Marlene.

"I forgot my notebook in the car," she said. "I'll be right back." She gave Zack a pointed look and prayed he would take a hint.

"I'll come with you." His casual abandonment of Marlene made her breathe a little easier.

As soon as they were out of earshot, he apologized. "I came as soon as Gordy let me know he wasn't going to be here. I'm sorry I'm late."

But Chloe wasn't listening to his words. Instead she beseeched the skies. "Oh, God. Get me out of this. I'll never lie again."

Zack stopped and firmly took her arm, halting her forward movement. "What did you lie about?"

The warmth of his hand penetrated her skin through her shirt, but she shook off the calm, protected feeling. "You can't stay. We'll have to cancel."

"Why? I'm here now."

"This isn't a lecture like I told Gordy. It's a hands-on class." She twisted her fingers together, finding it impossible to look into his trusting eyes. Why had she done this?

"Hands on?"

Chloe sucked in all the available oxygen. "It's a class to teach specific Kama Sutra positions. There are three other couples. You have to have a partner because everybody has sex."

Her words and her breath tumbled out as one.

Zack blinked, his eyebrows rose. "Having sex in a room with three other couples won't bother you?" His expression conveyed his shock at her brazenness.

Her cheeks heated. She glanced away, searching for an anchor to save her. When nothing appeared, she forced her gaze back to him. "Not really. It's educational. I'll need it for the future."

While his expression didn't change, his eyes twinkled. "I'm game if you are."

"No." She shook her head and clamped her hands onto his black t-shirt. "I can't have sex with a stranger for research."

He covered her hands with his. "I'm hardly a stranger." His deep voice soothed. Her anxieties eased with him in charge. Qualities Gordy lacked.

She pulled back, but Zack hooked an arm around

her waist and tugged her closer. Her brain ordered her to back up and force him to release her. Her body resisted doing anything of the sort. She longed to stretch against him like a cat and demand he stroke her skin.

"I don't know you." Her voice faded with her convictions.

"You know me. This can be our little secret. No one will ever suspect," he said solemnly. "But you and I, the three other couples, Marlene and the video tape."

"There's a video tape?"

"I made that up." Amusement edged his voice. "But I do think you're putting a fine point on the fact I'm a stranger, when you will be in a room full of strangers."

She thought about that for a minute. Her mind wasn't functioning at full capacity being pressed up against his muscular body. Like his tone, there was no yield to him.

This was all Gordy's fault. As usual he'd left her to clean up the problems. Well, this time she wasn't going to make everything right. And he'd never need to know. She glanced at Zack. Would he tell?

"If I agree, promise me you'll never tell Gordy."

"Cross my heart and hope to die." He drew an X over his heart.

She couldn't croak out more than a whisper. "I'm probably going to go to Hell for this."

"I think God saves Hell for more serious crimes." He coughed. Was he laughing? "You need to kiss me."

"What?"

"Sweetheart, you're as nervous as a virgin on prom night. In order to convince old Marlene that we're a couple, you need to relax and get used to my touch."

"Yeah. Right. Okay. Now?"

What if someone saw? She searched the tree-lined deserted street.

"Right now." He inched her firmer against him. "I've dreamed about kissing you."

"You have?"

His lips covered hers. Oh my God. Zack and Gordy didn't kiss the same way at all. Gordy gave quick pecks and Zack acted like she was a gourmet meal. He savored her. *And he'd dreamed about kissing her*.

Her eyes drifted shut as she gave up both control of her mouth and her mind. He supported her weight. Otherwise she would have melted onto the sidewalk.

The scent of orange blossoms surrounded her. She inhaled deeply. He'd used her soap. It smelled different on him. No doubt it was changed by the underlying scent of predator, a more powerful turn on than all the aftershave Gordy wore.

His kiss became more urgent as his rough hands boldly stroked her body. Unable to help herself, she moaned. He growled deep in his throat. The sound thrilled her.

The skin on her breasts stretched tight and when his hands covered them, she welcomed the relief and squirmed closer. Nor did she murmur a protest when he cupped her derriere, lifted her off the ground to grind against her. If she had any control over her body, she'd have thrown her head back and howled with pleasure.

It wasn't until one of his large hands slid between

her legs that she yelped. Zack drew back, panting. Chloe's eyes fluttered open. His hooded eyes conveyed a heat that had her trembling like a leaf in the wind. A deep chuckle escaped him only to disappear when she pulled him to her and nibbled his lips.

The sound from her throat was feral and untamed. A beast in her had been freed and a wild woman emerged. She wanted him. Her response pleased him. She could see it is his eyes.

Just when she was finally going after what she wanted, a momentary panic swamped her.

This was Gordy's brother. Where was her mind? If she raised a protest, she couldn't take the class. But the bigger crime was that if she raised a protest, she couldn't have Zack. She was going to Hell for sure. A low keening sound rose from her chest as he pinched her nipples.

"Are you a screamer?" he asked, his throaty voice sent ripples down her spine.

Was she?

She didn't know. With him, she might be.

Chapter Six

Marlene showed Zack and Chloe into a private curtained area to change. "I don't know if I've got a robe big enough to fit you." She eyed Zack. A wry, knowing smile curled her lips.

Did the woman have a subtle bone in her body? Probably not, considering what she did for a living. Although who was she to throw stones? Wasn't she going into the same business? Not to mention her action on the street just now. She was pretty sure sex in a public area was a crime.

Zack pulled the drapes firmly shut, providing the illusion of privacy.

Chloe turned her back and reached for the top button of her shirt. The three-way mirror caught her expression of triumph like a sly cat with everything but the yellow feathers hanging out of her mouth. For today at least, Zack was hers. Where was her mind? She shouldn't be this happy. But hiding her smile didn't change the rapid tattoo of her heart.

She pulled off her shirt and reached behind her to unfasten her plain white cotton bra. Zack unhooked it before she had a chance. His hands slid around her and captured her breasts. Squeezing gently.

"In the future," he whispered in her ear. "I like the low lacy kind that fastens in the front."

She swallowed hard and studied his face in the mirror. His eyes were closed. A very male look of supreme satisfaction played across his face. His fingers tweaked her nipples causing a flash of electricity to arc through her body.

"I'm too big," she whispered.

His eyes opened. "Sweetheart, you're perfect."

He bent his head and kissed her neck. The blood in her veins pulsed, sending shock waves throughout her system. If he kept doing that they'd never finish undressing. But she made no move to stop him even when she felt her panties moisten.

"Hurry up, you two." Marlene called through the curtain.

With another squeeze Zack released her breasts and dropped his hands to the button of her jeans. She'd read enough to know that her aroused scent was an aphrodisiac, but scent was one thing, she was dripping. An ache captured her feverish body.

Touch me. Please touch me.

Zack dropped to his knees and helped her shimmy out of her jeans and panties. With his hands holding her hips in place he rained kisses across the small of her back and down her buttocks.

The trip to hell would be worth it. One thing for certain, Zack didn't need to learn anything. He could probably teach this class.

Chloe forced herself to step away from him while she could still make her legs move.

# # #

Zack stared in the mirror. Group sex. Well, this'd be a first. And group sex with instructions. Something he'd never tell his team. They'd hoot and holler. Hell, he'd never live it down. If anybody but Chloe had asked, he would have refused. Right now it seemed too good to be true.

Maybe he'd write a book about it.

The black robes Marlene provided looked new. Chloe draped in silk looked sexy. Her long slender legs were smooth and called to his hands. He imagined caressing her soft skin and hearing her moan. Later, when they weren't under the class magnifying glass he'd let some of his fantasies take root.

"How much did this class cost?" Zack asked as he tugged his t-shirt over his head. The fabric whispered as she brushed by him leaving stirred up air and her sweet scent in its wake.

"Chloe?"

She'd poked her head out of the curtained enclosure, giving him a quick backward glance. "We need to hurry. They're ready to start."

Zack pulled his jeans and underwear down, and in a matter of seconds was naked. He reached for the flimsy robe just as Chloe ducked her head back inside. His fully aroused state was to be expected, but in the mirror he caught her staring.

Her mouth slightly open, her shallow breathing caused her chest to rise and fall quicker, her pale cheeks flushed. He restrained his urge to grab her, push up against the wall and take her hard. She was far enough gone that she wouldn't object and later he could romance her. But Marlene, the dragon woman awaited them.

This was going to be one sweet week.

Chapter Seven

Gordy rolled over and slapped Dixie on the butt. "Time to get up."

Dixie didn't move. Gordy struggled out of bed, headed toward the bathroom. As he passed the shower, he twisted the lever to hot and jerked it up. The pipes rumbled. Ice-cold water spurted into the stall until finally a smooth flow ran. It'd be several minutes before the hot water made its way from the heater in the garage. He needed the sound of running water to help him pee.

The man in the mirror frowned at him. He looked like hell. Not going to that class with Chloe was a relief. Facing her this morning and listening to a lecture on sex would've done him in. Too bad Zack wasn't around more.

One thing for sure he wouldn't have gotten the shit kicked out of him three nights ago by that redneck cretin, Dwayne Hollister. Maybe he'd sic Zack on him anyway. Zack would pound Dwayne's face to raw hamburger for messing with his baby brother.

Gordy paused and wondered one more time if Dwayne secretly worked for Bubba. His last meeting with Bubba hadn't gone well at all.

"Ya holding out on me?" Bubba had demanded as he thumbed through the money Gordy had given him. The heavy man's foot tapped impatiently on the gas pedal - gunning the engine.

"Hell, no." *Shit, did Bubba know something?*

"Word to the wise, race-boy. Don't let me find out ya are."

"I'd never do that." Had he believed him? Bubba

wasn't above doing whatever was necessary to keep his crew in line.

Steam poured out of the shower stall.

He stuck his head into the bedroom and yelled at Dixie one more time. "Get up. Now." Still she didn't move. Lazy bitch. He had been surprised to see her in his bed. He must have really been out of it. The last thing he remembered was saying goodbye to Zack.

Hot water beat down on him washing away the stench of tobacco and whiskey. How could one feel so weary at twenty-four? His stomach lurched, but he managed not to puke.

Closing his eyes he stood under the steaming water trying to recover some energy. Did he still have some crank? This was a day he could use a boost. A noise came from outside the shower. Dixie must be up. The water temperature changed from hot to scalding. He jumped back.

"Hey, what're you doing?" he yelled over the flushing toilet.

"Sorry, I forgot."

He shut off the water and opened the door. Steam fogged the mirrors. Probably just as well. He wasn't that pretty today anyway.

"What's your schedule?" Dixie asked from the bedroom.

"I've got a bunch of errands to run. Then I've got to stop by a class I was supposed to attend today. It ends at four. So I thought I'd show up about fifteen minutes before it was over."

"You want me to cook breakfast?"

"Nope, I've got to hit the road. You ready to go."

"Give me a minute, will ya? I just got up."

"I thought you had to pick up your daughter at pre-school," he said, rushing her.

"Not until two."

"It's a quarter of two now," he said, knowing full well it was only noon.

Dixie squealed. Gordy grinned. She'd be furious when she looked at a clock. Too bad he wouldn't be there to see it.

Chapter Eight

Chloe had fantasized about this class. A darkened room, lit by flickering candles, scented with rich, exotic incense and soothing music playing in the background, something classical and romantic. She'd expected to see artistic renderings and join an intellectual discussion about how various positions could be adapted to provide more stimulation and more excitement.

No one would expect her to take her clothes off in front of a bunch of naked strangers.

That dream was crushed when she entered the bright sunroom and suppressed a gasp of despair. Three other couples sat on cushioned mats scattered around the open room. Sunlight streamed through floor-to-ceiling glass windows. The hard beat of the background music had many of the couples keeping time.

She and Zack were the youngest. Most were well over forty and the bearded guy looked closer to sixty. As a therapist this would be her clientele. Dredging up a smile and throwing her shoulders back, she worked to project confidence.

No one smiled. No one paid any attention. Instead the group listened to the dark haired man seated furthest away. The words were too muted to hear. The group laughed. High, nervous, naughty laughter. Chloe could guess the direction of the man's story. The man leaned back, a barely suppressed smile of satisfaction on his face. His eyes flicked up to meet hers. He raised his eyebrows.

Chloe's chest tightened. Could she do this?

Could she have sex in a room full of strangers? Glancing over her shoulder at Zack didn't help. His face gave nothing away. But his hand resting on her waist gave her a gentle squeeze offering her courage.

Gordy would have embarrassed her by saying, just loud enough for others to hear, "You can't think I'm going to get it on in front of all these old farts." Zack may have had the same thought, but she didn't think so.

The music stopped. Marlene in a flurry of blue and green stood in front of the group. "Good. Everyone's ready."

Zack and Chloe reached the mat farthest from the door. "Stand up. We will begin with exercises."

Chloe almost sagged with relief. Exercising with robed strangers would be easy. Especially compared to what lay around the corner.

"Men, stand behind your partner and place your hands on her hips."

Zack's large warm hands enclosed her hips. She imitated the back and forth and side-to-side hip movements Marlene made. Awkwardness made her movements jerky. Zack stood close behind her. Touching her. Exhaling warm air that curled around her neck. Her cheeks flamed at his proximity and the suggestive movements.

Surreptitiously she checked out the other three women in the class. None of them seemed the least bit embarrassed. Chloe scolded herself. Focusing on the floor, she worked on relaxing.

Zack whispered in her ear. "This'd be more fun if I could bite your ass."

Chloe stumbled. Her movements faltered. Zack's strong hands kept her in place, preventing her from falling. She'd just about caught the rhythm when his whispered words reached her again. "Tonight we'll do this right."

Tonight? He thought they were continuing this? She couldn't have a torrid affair with Zack while he was home on vacation.

Could she?

Marlene changed the exercises. Now they did deep-knee squats. The short robes gaped open with every downward thrust. Chloe grabbed hers to keep it closed. When Marlene shifted the group to straight-leg toe touching, Chloe clamped her eyes shut. She heard Marlene's footsteps and wondered if the older woman was eyeing Zack's butt. If Chloe had been behind him, she would be.

# # #

When the exercises ended and everyone straightened, Zack saw Chloe eye the door and knew her thoughts were on escape. How had she ever decided on sex therapy as a career? She had more hang-ups than any woman he knew. And more contradictions. She'd signed up for a class, knowing what it entailed, and yet was terrified to be here.

Not just out of shyness or modesty, for her it was more, but what? She'd said her breasts were too big. What a stupid idea. Why hadn't his brother been worshiping at her flawless body? She was stunning and clueless. Well, if he did nothing else, he could ease her fears on that account.

As in all introductions each person was required to make a statement explaining he or she was here. He missed what the first couple had to say. It didn't matter.

The next woman stood up, a slender redhead,

late-forties. "I'm Helene. I'm here…," her lips curled in a sad smile "…because of my recent surgeries." The smile remained in place, but the heartbreak was in her voice.

"Last year I was diagnosed with breast cancer. To save my life I ended up having two radical mastectomies. Frank and I," she nodded toward her partner, the older bearded man still seated on the mat, "have struggled to revive the physical intimacy in our marriage."

As she spoke she unknotted the belt holding her robe together. The gown opened and a tattooed chest appeared before them. From the sides of her body, roses climbed, forming a trellis of multicolored flowers in full bloom across her chest.

Zack was a warrior. The horrors and mutilations he'd witnessed were a part of his life, but the sharp intake of breath that came from Chloe made him ache for her. He wrapped his arm around her waist and whispered, "She's gorgeous, isn't she?"

Chloe riveted her head to stare at him. "Do you think so?"

"Absolutely. Not only a beautiful body, but an indomitable spirit as well, hard combination not too admire."

She nodded, continuing to study his face. When it was her turn, she rose. "My name is Chloe La Ruse, graduate student. I plan to continue my studies at the Kinsey Institute at the University of Indiana next semester to become a sex therapist. This class offers techniques that would allow me to help others in the future."

She hesitated. "However--" For the first time, she looked at each face. Zack saw for her it was no longer a room of strangers. "I think I will benefit more than I ever imagined."

Other class members smiled and nodded.

Zack offered her a hand. "I came," he said without rising. "Because Chloe needed me."

"You didn't give your name," Alyssa, the woman on the next mat, said.

"Call me Gordy."

Marlene moved to her flipchart. Enlarged photographs of the original Kama Sutra drawings were positioned next to photographs of real-life couples in the same positions.

"We start with the misnamed missionary position because that is most familiar to everybody."

"An old hat," the dark haired man in the corner called out. Zack didn't remember his name. His partner laughed.

Marlene didn't bat an eye, but her lips drew into a grimace. "Perhaps an old hat, but universally loved. Why?"

"It's easy," the man said. "Missionaries were boring."

"No," Marlene faced off with the man. "Because it provides an important level of intimacy - eye contact."

Chloe bent her head over her notebook scribbling furiously. Next Marlene produced an anatomical drawing showing male insertion into the female. Zack sat amazed. He'd never imagined sex could be boring. Marlene droned on before finally turning the page.

"Unicorn's Horn," she said. "In this position, the female sits impaled on the male lap facing away from him. The advantage for the male is getting to watch his lover's buttocks move on his erection."

Zack had no trouble imagining sex with Chloe in a variety of exotic positions. The unicorn's horn looked more educational than erotic and more work than passion. If they got to choose which position they got to try, he'd pass on this one.

The other couple, Helene and Frank nodded. A lightning bolt of guilt hit Zack hard. If breasts were an issue, the unicorn horn would be a good choice. Chloe readjusted her position.

"You'll be more comfortable if you lean against me," he whispered. She moved to sit between his legs and used his chest for a back cushion.

Oh, yeah. This class isn't that bad.

Marlene went through about twelve drawings, describing each position thoroughly. Word for word Chloe wrote everything down, complete with stick figure replicas.

Occasionally, he'd make a comment to make her giggle or watch her blush.

Chapter Nine

After all her fretting, Chloe was amazed at how much she enjoyed the class with Zack. His comments relaxed her and her tension eased, until Marlene finally said, "Now we're to the good part."

Her heart jumped a beat maybe two. This was the career she'd chosen. In the future she'd see so many couples having sex it would be as the man said, "old hat." But right now apprehension held her in thrall.

Zack's hands caressed her arms. Big, strong, rough hands. She sat up straighter and inched away from him, making a pretense out of putting her notepad away when in fact the true reason was to put some distance between them. She crawled to the edge of the cushion.

"Good sex," Marlene said, "begins with kissing. Long, deep, slow, wet kisses that last three days according to Kevin Costner in that baseball movie."

All the other couples fell into kissing. Only Chloe was the holdout. What did Zack think?

He lay propped up on an elbow. His casual pose warred with the intense look in his eyes as he waited for her. He didn't give a rip about the class or Marlene or the impressions other's had. He only cared what she thought. Her decision. If she stood up and left right now, he'd be with her without condemnation, without judgment. At least, she thought so.

Next to her Alyssa moaned. Distracted, Chloe glanced at her neighbor. Alyssa was in a world of her own. No one cared what Chloe did.

Only Zack. Her tentative smile was met by his

outstretched hand. She uncurled. Lying side-by-side he was so much bigger than she was. It appealed to her feminine instinct. He stroked her cheek and jaw, rounding the nape of her neck. Slowly he drew her to him.

His touch brought stress. Not because it was Zack. Gordy would have made her just as miserable. She wasn't sure she was ready to have sex in front of others. Thousands of hours of classroom videos hadn't prepared her for this moment.

Chapter Ten

Kissing her was like falling into a cool mountain stream on a hot day. Zack angled his head to capture her lips and drank fully. She tasted better than he'd dreamed. That kiss by the car had been hot and ravenous. This one was to fill a man's desires.

Her body slowly molded to his.

Could he make love to her with someone looking on? Probably. But the way he wanted? No way. In the next several days he'd make up for lost time. If she wanted to believe it was for research. No problem. Then she and Gordy could go back to whatever bizarre arrangement they had concocted and he'd return to California.

No harm. No foul.

He rolled on top of her, wanting to open her robe, touch her skin and suck her pretty rose nipples. Pressing a knee between her legs he parted them enough he could nestle between. Her golden hair poured onto the mat like strands of gold glinting in the sun.

She raised her knees to allow her hips to cushion him. He was home.

"Just kissing," Marlene admonished.

That's all he was doing. Kissing. Kissing a woman he could kiss for the rest of his life. As quickly as the thought formed, he eased back and stared down at Chloe. Her tawny eyes had darkened and her lips were wet and swollen from his mouth.

He'd imagined her just like this.

But not as a permanent fixture in his life.

He was a SEAL. A love 'em and leave 'em, kind

of guy. Not a settling down, I'll-be-home-at-six-for-dinner-honey kind of guy.

Her lips curved in a sleepy smile. He unknotted the belt at her waist and slid his hand next to her cool skin and upward until his hand rested at the lower curve of her breast. His thumb picked up the rapid beat of her heart which perfectly matched his own. Her lids fluttered closed seducing him into believing the fantasy spread before him.

What had she said? Next semester. Graduate School. Indiana. She didn't expect him to stay.

His head lowered until he'd captured her mouth again and lost himself in its sweetness.

Alyssa on the next mat moaned loudly, followed by a muffled giggle. Someone cleared his throat. He raised his head to look. But it wasn't Alyssa who had problems.

Helene stood, tightening the belt on her robe. Tears streaked her face. "I can't do this. I thought I could, but I can't." Frank sat cross-legged on the mat with his head in his hands.

Chloe pushed against Zack's chest and obediently he rolled off of her exposing her skin. She snatched her robe together before she sat up. Her pink cheeks charmed him. When was the last time he'd been with a woman so shy?

"What exactly is the problem?" Marlene's voice was more caring than he'd believed was in her nature.

Helene gnawed her lower lip. "The problem is…." She took a long breath. "Frank misses my breasts."

Frank said nothing.

"Is that true, Frank?"

Frank raised his head. "Yeah, it is. I do miss your breasts. But you know what I miss more than your breasts? I miss your laughter. I miss the woman you used to be before the diagnosis. Before our lives went to hell in a hand-basket."

Helene looked thunderstruck.

"How do you expect our relationship to survive with you taking its pulse every fifteen minutes? Every word I utter, you search for hidden meanings. I'm so afraid of saying something wrong, I've given up trying."

Chloe appeared fascinated with the couple's problems. Zack leaned back on his elbows and studied the green lawn on the other side on the windows, the low bushes planted tight to the house to hide the red clay dirt backsplash that colored the concrete slab and several inches of brick. A weeping willow's branches hung gracefully almost to the ground.

Paneled glass windows lined three walls of the sunroom, opening onto an immaculately kept yard with a small cascading waterfall. A high wooden fence offered sufficient privacy.

He drummed his nails on the tile floor. Were they here for sex or therapy? If they ever got around to sex, Chloe should feel guilt-free; this truly was a research class.

Helene rejoined Frank on the mat. Both hugged and cried. Alyssa on the next mat also sniffled. Zack squirmed. Sex wasn't supposed to be emotional.

"Let's take ten minutes and start fresh," Marlene suggested. "There's bottled water in the hall."

"Would you like some water?" Chloe asked.

"Sure." Zack stretched out on the mat. What he wanted was to get on with this.

As she left the room, Marlene glided toward him, her flowing gown sweeping the floor. Her eagle eyes skimmed his body, assessing his state of arousal. "Impatient, are we?"

He shrugged.

"It's interesting what you learn from teaching a class like this. For instance, you and Chloe don't act like you've been together for almost eight years."

"Really?"

"No, you're much too… Shall we say frisky?"

When Zack had agreed to the class, he hadn't anticipated the crying or even the horny old lady watching them. But he wasn't planning to let her dish shit, no matter how much Chloe revered her. "That's what she loves best about me."

Marlene lips formed a sly smile. "I'm looking forward to your report next week."

"I'll try to be detailed." Zack raised an eyebrow. He had no idea what report Marlene was talking about, but he figured her real object was to yank his chain. *Yank away, honey.*

Marlene reminded him of every Chief he'd met in the Navy. Every one of them wanted control. When the first couple reentered the room and headed toward the flip chart to study some of the drawings, Marlene's interest in Zack disappeared and she zipped across the room to intercept them. He smiled, knowing his joy at her absence would be temporary at best.

Why had Gordy sent him to this class? He'd known the type of class it was. Maybe not the actual intimacy, but he certainly understood Chloe's interests. Zack shifted uncomfortably. His brother had pushed him into an untenable situation and he'd gone for it. Big time.

He'd lusted after Chloe. Now that he'd touched her and seen her naked, he wanted to be with her more than ever. But his own hang up was his baby brother.

Alyssa and Chloe entered the room together and headed in his direction. Chloe handed him the bottle of water as both women dropped gracefully to their separate mats. Zack twisted the cap and took a long swig to clear his head and wash away his guilt.

"You've got great breasts," Alyssa whispered. "Who did them?"

Zack choked and narrowly prevented spitting water all over the women. Chloe blushed crimson.

"I'm sorry I've embarrassed you," Alyssa said.

Opening her robe, she displayed her own breasts. Zack wanted to singe his eyes with hot pokers to erase the picture of a woman older than his mother, displaying her surgically enhanced breasts.

He was expected to admire them and maybe make flirting noises about including Alyssa in their play, but he couldn't do it. This was someone else's script, not his. Zack got where he was by making his own moves.

He stood up. "I'm going to the restroom," he said, leaving Chloe to deal with Alyssa's bare breasts.

No wonder his brother hated these things. What the hell was he doing here anyway?

Chapter Eleven

Once he'd met with Bubba, Gordy would still have time to hit the training track and make a few laps before he had to be at Chloe's class. He gunned his engine in anticipation.

"Easy there, big boy." He chuckled and patted the dash as he drove toward the airbase.

For the most part, Bubba worked out of his truck. With all the money the fat guy hauled in, he could at least get a decent truck instead of the old, battered dark green wreck he drove. But Bubba, not the most patient of guys, had revved the engine enough times. There was more under the hood than the standard factory model.

The former linebacker was not an original thinker. He'd gotten to where he was by developing a system and sticking to it. Every day of the week he worked different parking lots moving from one to another. He didn't trust cell phones. Rather than the radio he listened to a police scanner all day in his truck.

As Gordy entered the parking lot, he saw the gnarly green truck in the usual spot near the far exit. Without stopping he exited at the far side and ten minutes later pulled into the B&L and circled around to the back by the dumpsters. Bubba was five minutes behind him.

"This it?" The fat man sneered at the envelope holding the money Gordy handed him.

"Yeah. Every penny's there."

Bubba tossed the envelope through the cab window of his truck and unlocked the aluminum tool chest. He scanned the neighborhood and the lot for several minutes.

"I don't know why we do all this dancing around. The cops aren't watching you." Gordy said.

"You ain't the one in charge, buddy boy," Bubba handed him a stuffed manila envelope.

"Why can't we just pay the cops off? Then we won't have to worry."

"Ya can't be as dumb as ya act," Bubba said. "This'll take ya through Saturday."

"Maybe longer. My sister's wedding is this weekend. My time's going to be tied up."

Bubba frowned. "Ya got more excuses for not working than anybody I know."

"Hell, I work all the time for you."

Bubba snorted. "That's why you're barely dragging minimum. Another bad week, race-boy, and I'll give someone else your route. Then see how fast ya lose that sporty car when ya can't keep up the payments."

"I told you, those problems are behind me. I got a lawyer taking care of it."

Bubba half closed his eyes and shook his head, like listening to Gordy's excuse was too much to bear. He lumbered back to his truck, climbed in and drove off.

Damn. The big oaf bummed him out. He pulled open an orange plastic container and popped another couple of pills. Once he ran the course a few times, he'd unwind. The convenience store was out of Lone Star, so he'd picked up a six-pack of Budweiser instead and had it tucked behind the seat. Arthur wouldn't let him on the track if he thought he'd been drinking. Twisting the cap off, Gordy took a big swig and then laughed out loud. What Arthur didn't know wouldn't hurt him.

# # #

The hunch of Zack's shoulders as he left the room told Chloe, he wasn't happy. She frowned at Alyssa. "Cover up. I don't want to see your boobs or your boob job. This isn't show and tell."

An embarrassed laugh escaped Alyssa as she pulled her robe over her breasts. "You sound like a teacher."

"I am a teacher, but I just realized I've been acting like a fool. And that's coming to a stop right now." Chloe grabbed her notebook, rose off the ground, purposely retightened the belt on her robe and strode after Zack.

She pushed by a frowning Marlene as she left the room. Zack stood alone halfway down the hallway. His casual stance belied the tightness in his shoulders and the unhappiness in his dark brown eyes. This man wasn't Gordy. She studied his rugged, hard features and knew she'd dishonored him, both by refusing to acknowledge the truth of who he was and by taking advantage of his kindness. He allowed her to treat him like a puppy on a leash because that's how she treated Gordy. But he wasn't a puppy and while he may have tolerated that behavior in the short run, it was only because he wanted to have sex with her. And she'd known it deep inside since the funeral. Not acknowledging the facts didn't make them less true.

Right now he was trying the oldest trick in the book and she'd not only bought into it, she'd encouraged it. Men, like Zack, couldn't be controlled. They saw. They took. They conquered.

Oh, he could wait patiently like he was doing now, bide his time pretending compliance, until she lowered her guard. How many stories had she read about the fox guarding the hen house, or the wolf in sheep's clothing or even the Greeks and Trojan horse?

If you didn't understand history you were destined to repeat it. Some professor had said that in one of her history classes. She didn't remember which one and she didn't care, but she would stop being an idiot now. Her career was not the be-all to end-all. It certainly wasn't worth sacrificing her personal ethics.

"Are you ready to go?"

Zack straightened, studied her eyes. "Yeah, I am."

"Let's hit the road." She walked down the hall to the curtained area she'd used as a dressing room, pleased that her clothes were still scattered about. Zack entered behind her.

Neither spoke as they sorted garments. Chloe carefully avoided looking in his direction. Without knocking, Marlene stuck her head in between the flaps of the drapes.

"What are you two doing? We're ready to re-start."

"We're leaving," Zack said.

"Why?"

Chloe was surprised Marlene's voice sounded so startled. She would have thought the fact they were dressing would have been a major clue.

"Because this class isn't right for us," Chloe said, turning toward the drape as she buttoned her shirt. Zack's eyes met hers. She wondered briefly what he was thinking.

Marlene's head swiveled back and forth between them. She didn't miss the slight smile Zack gave Chloe. "I'm not refunding your fifteen hundred dollars."

Zack's encouraging smile disappeared. He opened his mouth to speak, but Chloe jumped in first. "Fine. Keep it." Her jeans were still on the floor and she bent to pick them up.

Marlene stepped fully inside the dressing room. She lowered her voice, attempting to be authoritative. "You knew what this class was about when you signed up."

"Yes," Chloe agreed. "It was 'the voyage of self-discovery' if I can quote your brochure. We discovered that it wasn't the direction we wanted to go."

"Are you trying to ruin my business?"

Zack sat down on the chair and bent over to put on his socks.

Chloe faced Marlene. "I doubt I have that power. Don't you have a six-month waiting list?"

For some reason that thought calmed Marlene. She took a deep breath. "Why don't we compromise? I'll refund half your money and you'll agree not to tell people you were unhappy."

Chloe looked at Zack who watched her face. She wanted to tell Marlene to stuff it, not because it was the older woman's fault. She had no one to blame but herself. But turning down seven hundred - fifty dollars was foolhardy when she needed that money for her PhD.

She nodded. "Okay."

"Fine. I'll send you a check tomorrow." Marlene said. "I have to get back to the rest of the class now. I can't remember a group that's been this difficult."

As soon as they were outside, Zack turned to her and asked incredulously, "You spent FIFTEEN HUNDRED DOLLARS on that class? When you needed to get your car fixed?" He grabbed her arm and started propelling her toward his vehicle.

"I was thinking of the future."

"Where'd you get that kind of money?"

She was offended. What business of it was his? But she told him anyway. "Gram. I live off my part-time teaching income, but any extra money comes from the money I got from selling Gram's house."

He opened the passenger door and pushed her inside. "What made you change your mind?" he asked as he slid into the driver's seat.

"I wasn't willing to sell my soul to have sex with you."

He stared at her for several minutes, his face blank by design. Finally, he turned the key in the ignition never taking his eyes from her. "Good."

Chapter Twelve

Gordy rolled his head from side to side. His neck and shoulders no longer ached, but his skin itched like mad. He resisted giving in to the scratching. From experience he knew once he started, it never quit. Damn crank always affected him this way. His time on the track hadn't been his best time, but he'd run it with precision.

"You looked good out there today," Arthur said when Gordy stepped into his cool office to settle up his bill. The office was a small portable metal building that housed a counter, a computer and a television. Every sports' station and car race was picked up and televised by the disk set on constant play. If nothing good was on, Arthur popped in old races and ran them. Today baseball spring training sprinted across the giant screen. Mark McGuire was at bat.

Gordy watched McGuire swing and miss. "Yeah."

Arthur was about the only friend he had who knew how desperately he wanted to race. Thirty years ago Arthur had wanted it just as badly himself. Enough he'd built a track in middle of nowhere to qualify drivers for a racing license. When north Texas didn't produce enough want-a-bes, Arthur diversified. He taught driver's education, trained police to drive in high-speed chases and adverse circumstances, and let young hot-roders perfect their skills. Zack had spent countless hours here years before.

The parched Texas prairie dotted the landscape with red clay, grubby mesquite trees and the perpetual clicking pump jacks. It was a land where only the tough survived. The weather prided itself on being extreme. Mainly it was hot and dry, but when cold, the misery mounted. Ice storms blanketed an entire region in sheets of slick glass. As little as an inch of snow and the entire town came to a halt. And on those occasions when it rained, a gentle sprinkle was less likely than a deluge. How could a town that fought drought every summer still flood at least once a year?

In the middle of it all sat the twenty-five acres of man-made obstacles and ribbons of concrete that had kept Gordy from losing his mind.

Arthur scowled. "What're you on?" His eyes searched Gordy's face.

"Nothin."

"Bull hockey. I'm not telling you again. Don't come in here drinking and doing drugs."

"I'm clean."

"Final warning. Next time, I'll ban you for life."

"I took something for a headache this morning that's all."

Arthur snorted. "Kid, grow up. If your dad was alive, he'd tell you the same thing. I suspect I know how you were able to buy a two hundred and fifty thousand dollar car, but that won't wash here. Clean up your act. Or don't come back."

Gordy stormed to the car, slamming the office door behind him. *Stupid prick.* The old man didn't know anything. He grabbed a Bud from behind the seat.

Purposely laying rubber, he wheeled onto the main road. The car fishtailed slightly. When the rear end straightened, he released one hand from the wheel and pulled the orange pill container out of his jacket pocket.

The fingerless leather racing gloves prevented him from reaching into the small opening. Cursing, he overturned the container onto the passenger's seat, grabbed two capsules and washed them down with warm beer. Everybody was on his ass. Zack would help him. He could talk to Arthur and get everything straightened out. It was three-fifteen now. If he hurried, he could still make it to Chloe's class by three-forty-five.

The four-way stop caught him by surprise. He blew through the stop sign and heard a long horn blow. Laughing, he lowered his window and stuck his hand above the car. Flying the one finger flag for that loser to see. The speedometer inched above one-hundred-twenty as he let the engine unwind. A Ferrari was built for speed.

# # #

"What exactly is your relationship with Gordy?" Zack wanted a straight answer.

"It's complicated." Chloe looked out the passenger window. Her hands clenched together in her lap.

"Because?" He prompted. His mouth tightened into a grim line. He should have gotten to the bottom of this before now. Where was his brain? He glanced at his lap, shifted uncomfortably in his seat and decided there was no need to investigate that question.

"We have history."

Zack wanted to bang his head against the steering wheel. Why were they going around Robin Hood's barn to get to what he wanted to know? "I don't care about your history. I want to know what relationship you have today."

"Let's just say we've drifted apart."

Another answer that told him nothing. "When did this start?"

Chloe studied her fingernails. "About the time he quit college. I wanted him to stay in school, but all he wanted was to follow in your footsteps."

Momentarily his exasperation dissipated. His chest filled with pride. Gordy wanted to be like him? And she wanted him to stay in college? "He wanted to join the Navy?"

"No, he wanted to drive for NASCAR. Classes meant nothing to him. He flunked out because he spent all day at that stupid driving track. Practicing, practicing, practicing. Every evening he spent hours at the computer trying to figure out how to get a sponsor."

"Why didn't he tell me? I might have been able to come up with some old contacts."

"Really," she said, sounding annoyed. "You can't be this obtuse. He couldn't ask you because it would smack of big brother getting him the job. He needed to do this on his own."

"All I could have gotten him was a foot in the door. How he did after that was up to him."

She shrugged. "The combination of my being still in school and him unemployed killed us. The job he wanted either wasn't available or he couldn't get it. We still hung out together, but only out of habit."

He nodded.

"When Gram died, I thought we'd just drift apart. We agreed to see other people. Except every now and then he'd show up on my doorstep."

"Why?"

"Sometimes even Gordy needs down time."

Didn't that just say it all? Zack had been a loner and Gordy was never without his posse. Even as a young kid, he was always in a group. Always stirring up trouble. He laughed, his tone a harsh staccato sound. "Who's he hanging with now?"

"I don't know his friends. Mainly he spends time at the B&L."

"And drives a Ferrari. He must be making some money. What kind of job does he have?"

He knew, or at least thought he did. But did she?

She shifted in her seat, rubbing her forehead with her fingers as she crossed her legs. Then she re-crossed her legs and massaged her temples. The third time she squirmed, he placed a firm hand on her knee. She looked at him.

She shrugged, "I've never asked. He's never said."

She wasn't clueless; she'd just turned a blind eye because she no longer cared. They truly had separated. "Why are you still together?"

Chloe was quiet for several minutes before she finally spoke. "Without Gordy, I have no one."

"Are you telling me that a girl who looks like you can't attract another boyfriend?"

"It's not that guys don't ask me out, but when you teach sex-ed classes men look at you differently. A lot of guys are interested in only one thing."

Well, yeah, he could see that. And it was the same thing he was interested in. Gordy had been safe for her. "Where is he now?"

"I don't know. I can try and call on the cell, but don't expect him to answer."

"Why?"

"He always avoids me when he thinks I'm

angry."

"Try him anyway."

She dug in her purse, pulled out her phone and dialed Gordy's number. Just as she predicted, no one answered.

# # #

Chloe wanted to be alone. She needed time to sort out her complex relationships with the Pritchard brothers. But with Zack staying at her house, it would be difficult to have any private time.

He pulled up in front of her apartment, put the car in park, but left the engine running. "Loan me your cell phone. I'll be back."

"Okay." Her momentary disappointment confused her. Hadn't she just wanted to get rid of him?

He leaned across her to open the door. "I can't make love to you until I know for sure that Gordy thinks you've broken up."

Chloe stared unable to believe his words. "What? I agreed to sex for the class alone. Research."

Zack chuckled and twisted his head to kiss her. Immediately her blood simmered and her will dissolved. Not meaning to encourage him, but unable to help herself, she leaned in closer for a deeper taste. Disengaging, he murmured in her ear. "You're in my system. And you've got me in yours. Exorcism is mandatory."

Chloe reached for the door handle. "We won't be making love," she said, rising from the car seat. "Sex without affection is just flesh rubbing together."

His laugh surprised her. He rarely laughed aloud. He smiled and occasionally chuckled. But this belly laugh was so infectious, she almost grinned in return.

"Oh, sweetheart," he said when he took a breath. "You have so much to learn."

Now he treated her like an ignorant child. Her indignation flared. "Well, I doubt if you'll be the one to teach me, if you have to ask your brother for permission." She slammed the car door. Refusing to look back, she stomped up the steps to her apartment. The distant sound of his laughter trailed like a shadow behind her.

Chapter Thirteen

Despite Zack's amusement, he wasn't sure why he had such a pressing need to find his brother. Chloe was wrong. He wasn't asking Gordy's permission. It was obvious from the way both of them behaved that their relationship was long over.

So his brother wanted to drive for NASCAR? Zack still had some contacts. Gordy would need to prove himself in the Busch Series first, but it would be just the thing to get his life straightened out. In six months with rigorous work and a change of scenery, Riggers and the unsavory lifestyle his brother had adopted would be a distant memory.

He hadn't the faintest idea where to look, but he had four potential locations. The first was Gordy's home. He flipped open his wallet and found the slip of paper his mother had sent with his new address.

Zack had been well suited for the SEALs long before he got there. Growing up in the prairie pitted man against the environment from his earliest childhood. The SEALs challenged him but when the going got tough he remembered what growing up in north central Texas had been like.

Gordy's garage sat open and empty. The dark house looked decrepit, in need of serious repair. How could his brother drive a Ferrari and live in a dump? Rather than go by his mother's house, he phoned. Glyn answered.

"Have you heard from Gordy?" he asked after they'd chatted for a few moments.

"No. We've been trying to find him for the last hour. He missed this afternoon's tux-fitting appointment."

No doubt that was high on Gordy's list.

"I'll try Chloe," Glyn offered.

"Don't bother. He's not there. I'll go by Arthur's."

"If you find him, let me know so I can kill him."

Zack chuckled. "Will do". But before Arthur's he wanted to drive by the B&L and see if Gordy spent his daylight hours in a bar in addition to those after dark.

The complexion of the town had changed. Hard working, hard living oil and cattle country was still boom and bust. During the good years, money flowed like oil spurting out of the ground. But it'd been years since the last oil boom had revitalized the county and the changes were significant.

The downtown hung on by a thin thread. Boarded up stores and deserted streets marked the lifeless area. Zack was grateful to get out when he had. He loved his danger-filled life. If he'd stayed here, his death would have been both slow and pitiful. No wonder his brother was sinking fast.

Scattered cars decorated the sparsely filled parking lot of the bar. Zack wasted half an hour quizzing the bartender about Gordy's whereabouts. He'd have gotten more information and a lot less hassle if he'd written Ann Landers.

Getting Gordy out of this town had become his number one priority. Well, that... and Chloe...

Chapter Fourteen

Zack circled the small lot adjacent to Chloe's apartment building. Every spot occupied. Resigned he drove on and found a parking space on the street two blocks away. Midnight had come and gone. The wasted evening frustrated him. No one had seen Gordy.

His mother's house had been a furor of last minute wedding preparations. He'd exited almost as quickly as he'd entered. His final trip to the B&L was as worthless as his first. He'd run out of time to get to Arthur's and had called instead.

Yep, Gordy had been there. Yep, Gordy had left. It wasn't until Zack asked about Gordy's state that Arthur gave him more than a flip answer. Zack sighed. Still no sign of his brother.

The windows of Chloe's apartment were dark. Would she be waiting up for him and would she enter his bedroom like she had the night before? When she opened the door, he'd lain there, debating the wisdom of turning over and lifting his covers to welcome her into his bed.

Tonight he would definitely roll over. In fact that wasn't even going to be an issue because her room was his first stop. And with any luck his last.

He slid his key in the lock. The door remained bolted. Chloe had set the dead bolt.

His lips kicked upward as he looked forward to seeing sparks fly. With Chloe's looks men would always give in to her without any qualms. She needed a man who challenged her. Not someone she could lead around by the nose. With a small amount of juggling, the deadbolt gave in under a minute. That lock was designed to keep out the mice. Even without his skills, one swift kick would knock the hollow-core door off its hinges.

As he crossed the room he unbuttoned his shirt and caught a whiff of lingering tobacco smoke from the B&L. Shower? He sniffed again. Definitely. Women saw a difference between dirty sex and stinky sex. No need to give her more ammunition than necessary.

# # #

Wearing her only nice nightgown, the one with a plunging lacy neckline, Chloe sat up in bed and debated her options. Zack was sneakier than she'd imagined. Silly her, thinking a deadbolt would keep him out.

Should she burst into the bathroom and demand to know how he got in? Or lock her bedroom door and force a chair underneath? Did she even own a chair that would work?

Pretending to be asleep would make her look like a nincompoop. If she propped herself against the headboard and waited for him, what would she do if he chose his own room instead?

So far he wasn't following her script at all. When Zack discovered the deadbolt was in place, he should've banged on the door. Reluctantly she would have allowed him to persuade her to open the door. As she stood before him in her seductive pale peach nightgown she would have calmly detailed the reasons why sex was not possible.

He'd beg and plead, but she'd stand firm. If he grabbed her, she'd resist -- to a point.

No, no, a thousand times no.

Okay, maybe not with so much melodrama. But

she wouldn't just say yes because he was in her house. Chloe La Ruse, America's sweetheart was not easy.

The shower stopped. She still didn't have a plan. Rolling to the edge of the bed, she groped blindly for the lamp. Her elbow slid, her hand jerked and the lamp sailed noisily to the floor. Panicked Chloe leaped out of bed caught her feet in the hem of the nightgown and tumbled headfirst into her nightstand. Instant pain. "Ow!"

Lights blazed as the overhead fixture came to life.

"Are you okay?" Zack asked, crossing the short distance between the door and her sprawled body in four steps. "Did you fall out of bed?" He crouched beside her. Beads of water glistened on his naked shoulders and his wet hair curled around his neck.

"I'm fine," she mumbled, struggling to sit up. Was he completely naked? No, he had one of her towels wrapped low around his waist.

"Wow, that's going to be some goose egg." Tenderly he touched his fingers to her forehead where she'd hit the nightstand. Chloe winced.

"I'm fine," she repeated, but didn't move from his arms.

"What were you doing?"

"A noise startled me," she lied. "When did you get here?"

"Just now," he answered absently as he continued to prod the lump on her forehead.

"Did you find Gordy?"

His deep brown eyes met hers. "No."

"No?" Did that mean no sex? She frowned.

Zack scooped her off the floor and placed her gently in the bed. The lamp, miraculously still intact, was returned to the table. She waited, her blood raced with excitement slowed to a pathetic crawl when he flipped off the light and closed the door almost shut. She swallowed hard. Once again her lack of coordination had cost her.

The light from the hallway angled onto the floor. She heard him moving around in the bathroom. Running water, the opening and closing of drawers, the sharp click of the hall light, the darkness. Chloe sat alone in her bed.

Well, that hadn't gone at all like she wanted.

She pouted and crossed her arms over her chest thinking about her options. The first indication she wasn't alone came when the mattress gave.

"Zack?" She could smell him now. Shampoo, orange blossom soap and predator. "What are you doing?"

Like she couldn't figure this one out.

"Getting comfortable."

"In my bed?"

"No," he said quietly as he scooted closer. "In your arms."

Chloe wanted to protest, to follow an outline she'd devised in her imagination. He stretched out beside her. Apparently, he'd left his towel behind. All the words she practiced in her head abandoned her.

This had to be wrong, but it felt so right when his arms encircled her and pulled her close. Would he kiss her? Long slow deep wet kisses that lasted for three days? Was it bad to hope he would?

"Pretty nightgown."

Her throat was parched. Nervously she licked her lips. His hand grazed her arm then traveled lightly over her hips. Her response of 'this old thing' was on the tip of her tongue, but before she could roll the words out, he said, "I think we should take it off."

"Take it off?" she croaked.

"Uh-huh." He tugged at the hem. "Lift up." Was she ready to be naked? Apparently, she was because she shifted as he commanded.

"Much better."

In the darkened room his lips honed in, finding her effortlessly without light. How could a man be so hard everywhere and have such gentle lips? How could such calloused hands stroke her so tenderly? How could a man with a reputation for speed move so slowly?

So much for standing firm, refusing sex. She hadn't uttered a sound. Now with him touching her, she couldn't think of a word to say. Thank goodness this wasn't the Jeopardy Show.

I'll take orgasms for two thousand, Alex. Please let this be a daily double.

His knees pressed between her legs separating them and giving him space to roll on top of her. Alive with sensation, her awareness of Zack affected her on every level. His touch sent sparks flying and emotions churning. It'd be so easy to surrender, but she couldn't allow herself that luxury.

This sex was strictly for research with a man who'd never planned to stay. He'd leave and never look back. But he made her feel so treasured, so wanted, so special. She felt girly, delicate and feminine. A primitive side existed that made her want to lose control, to let him take charge and protect her.

Could she be a bigger fool?

Sunday tops, he'd be gone. But tonight she would pretend he wasn't leaving. For tonight, he'd be hers. She wouldn't let herself fantasize about the future. Chloe sank deeper into the kiss. Her body responded without any encouragement.

Her skin itched and shrank until it was too tight. Her nipples ached, hard with need. The pull of desire surged between her legs. Her pulse pounded with need.

When he touched her she bit her lips to keep from howling in delight. She shifted hoping he'd fondle her deeper, whisper erotic thoughts. He broke the kiss. She needed more.

Circling his neck with her arm she brought those wicked lips to her breasts, straining for his attention.

The light brush of his hand between her legs had her arching. His clever fingers dipped and swirled, but it wasn't until he stroked her clitoris that she screamed, "Oh my God, do that again."

A muffled sound came from Zack whose mouth still feasted on her nipple. She assumed he was amused, but still he obliged her request. Like a wound up toy whose spring was tightened one time too often, she came apart in his hands.

Unable to roust any energy, she collapsed on the bed while he rose above her and tore open the foil pack.

Thank you for making this worthwhile. More than worthwhile. Good. Really, really good.

He lifted her legs over his broad shoulders. And inched into her. He was big. Huge. Like a mountain of a man trying to get through a thimble opening.

"Easy," he murmured. "We're going to go slow."

She strained her legs against his chest trying to push him back. Zack's thumb circled between her legs. Her attention focused on his actions. Tightness and anticipation curled her toes. Incoherent noises erupted from her throat.

"Now," he murmured. "Come for me now."

As though she'd been waiting for his instruction, Chloe fell over the edge. Everything in her coiled and then exploded. She needed Zack.

Inside. Now.

He pushed against her until she was full. Tight, but not painful. She wiggled to have the feel of him.

That little trick with the thumb was worth remembering. That'd be something to help her patients. Oh God, she needed to make notes. She almost scrambled to a sitting position, but he caught her with his voice.

"Stay with me."

"I'm here."

"No, you're not. You're a million miles away." He leaned forward and kissed her, but his kiss turned commanding, his tongue thrust in tempo with the rest of his body.

She couldn't breathe. She couldn't move.

Finally, she yanked her head away. "Faster," she whispered.

The rough growl of his throat was enough to have her quivering with uncontrolled lust, but the rumble sliced her like an erotic sword.

"Do you want me to fuck you really hard?" he whispered.

Oh yeah, she did.

He shifted his position and pounded into her. Her blood surged. A guttural groan from the depths of hell echoed in her ears as he jack hammered into her. Was it him? Was it her? Did it matter? Breathing became secondary.

Red lights flashed behind her closed eyes. Everything went black.

"Are you still with me?" he asked.

Gingerly, she opened her eyes. The bedroom lamp glowed. "I'm here," she mumbled and struggled to a sitting position.

"I brought you some water." He held out a glass.

"I passed out?" she asked when the realization hit her. "Damn, you must be the best lover in the world." Her mouth stretched in a wide, very pleased grin. "I passed out," she repeated with pride.

He smiled and lightly kissed her lips before taking her glass from her. Rather than placing it on the bedside table he returned it to the bathroom turned out the light and snuggled up against her in bed.

Within a matter of seconds Chloe's gentle breathing deepened and relaxed as she drifted into a sound sleep. Zack lay awake, trying to piece together his day. He found himself strangely disappointed in Chloe's response. Not the passing out part. The sex had been phenomenal. He was amazed he hadn't passed out. But her comment bothered him.

All the tricks and technique in the world couldn't duplicate that reaction with just any lover. First time sex was rarely as satisfying this had been.

Gordy's words came back to haunt him. "I feel like a freakin' lab rat." Were he and his brother more alike than he imagined?

Chapter Fifteen

Chloe opened her eyes exactly at five am. An annoying habit but especially today when the weight of Zack's arm lay around her waist. If she could slide out of bed without waking him, she'd surprise him with breakfast. Late yesterday she'd shopped with feeding him in mind.

Toast, bacon and eggs. A manly breakfast. She'd even indulged in good coffee with hazelnut flavoring.

She shifted. He rolled, freeing her body from the entrapment of his arm. The wadded up nightgown lay on the floor, but she stepped over it, preferring a pair of gym shorts and a baggy t-shirt.

By the time he awoke she'd have breakfast mainly done. The antiquated coffeemaker hissed and bubbled, sluggishly filling the pot.

Her cell phone rang. She snatched it off the charging station as quickly as she could.

"Hello."

Sobs greeted her. "Is Zack with you?" Glynnis asked.

"Hold on, let me see if he's awake." Chloe wanted to ask what had brought on the tears, but figured she'd hear soon enough. Maybe they were calling off the wedding. Since she hadn't been invited, she was strangely dispassionate.

He sat on the edge of the bed. Apparently her choice of wardrobe didn't thrill him based upon his raised eyebrow. She glanced in the mirror after she handed him the phone. Okay, not that cute.

He grunted into the phone. Then said, "Wait. I can't understand you. Say that again."

Chloe returned to the kitchen and poured him cup of coffee.

He spoke urgently into the phone. "I'll leave right now. Chloe's got a cell phone. We'll call from there."

He nodded his thanks at the coffee and holding his hand over the receiver, whispered, "Get dressed."

Chloe opened the closet door and heard him say, "Tell me exactly where I'm going. I'm sure I can find it."

She pulled a pair of slacks and a jacket out of the closet. Zack stood, picked up the coffee mug and took a long sip. He knitted his brow together and grimaced.

"I'll call you as soon as I'm there," He promised a final time and hung up the phone. "What's the weird flavor in your coffee?"

"Hazelnut. You don't like it?"

"It's fine."

"I can make regular coffee."

"No time, we need to go."

"I've got classes to teach today."

"Gordy's been in an automobile accident out on Highway 369. The police are already at the scene. Loan me your cell phone. I'll go alone."

"An accident? Is he hurt? I'll go with you. We can call the dean on the way."

She quickly discarded the slacks for jeans and a cropped sweatshirt, grabbed her purse and the camera sitting on the bookcase.

Chapter Sixteen

There wasn't a chance in hell they'd get close to the wreck. Traffic was backed up for miles. Who knew a nowhere two-lane back road around Riggers had so many vehicles on it this early in the morning?

Zack drummed his hands on the steering wheel and watched the traffic inch forward. For a man who spent hours waiting for the right time to strike, his patience had abandoned him.

Unable to delay even a second longer, he said, "Slide over here. I'm going on foot. When you find a place to park, pull over and I'll meet you at the accident site."

She thrust a small silver camera at him. "It's digital."

The early morning air cooled his heated skin as he sprinted between cars. Things had changed since he was last on this road. The cattle ditch - traditionally rough ground, weeds and a minor hole in the ground - now held a deep concrete culvert that ran the length of the highway on either side of the road.

He eyed the narrow thoroughfare as a possible throughway for speed but continued on the edge of the road, not wanting to miss anything, changing to the middle when traffic slowed.

He'd run about a mile before flashing lights were visible ahead. Orange cones narrowed the roadway to one lane leaving room for the ambulance, several police cars and a tow truck. Gordy's car wasn't visible. Other vehicles blocked the view.

As the traffic shifted into the opposite lane to be directed around the accident, Zack saw the tire marks.

They started a long way from the scene of the accident. The camera was a good idea.

He touched the pavement and ran a fingernail through the tire marks. A hunk of black rubber remained under his nail.

He moved to the edge of the road and peered down the culvert. The Ferrari was wedged nose down into the concrete. All he could see was the undercarriage pointing straight toward heaven and the scarred concrete that mapped the vehicle's journey. His stomach lurched. For the car to be positioned vertically, the entire front had to be caved in. He bet the inside of the vehicle had more folds than an accordion. Could Gordy have survived this? The car angled sharply in the ditch. Every inch of movement brought the painful sound of scraping metal.

Running to get closer was fruitless. If Gordy was wedged in the car they couldn't open the doors to get him out until the car was removed from the culvert. A wrench and chain were being attached to the rear axle. Zack forced himself to snap a couple of pictures.

One of the police officers waited beside the tow truck, holding the Jaws of Life, designed to pry the doors off the smashed vehicle. He wished that boded well, but suspected the worst. If his brother lived, it'd be a miracle. Although the miracle might have happened if Gordy had been thrown free. He slowed. Each step weighted with dread.

Across the road, a large group of pedestrians roped off by the police were herded together. If he ventured any closer, they'd force him to join that group. He refused to be part of the gawkers.

The culvert, a wide flared v with a four-foot flat bottom was lined with thick concrete to hold a torrent of water. Every fifty feet or so concrete footholds were notched into the side.

The nearest one was about twenty feet back. He jumped into the culvert, landing lightly. He didn't need the footholds, but Chloe might.

Using his arms for leverage he scaled the far side as easily as getting out of a bathtub. A dilapidated barbwire fence barricaded the barren grazing field beyond the culvert. He leapt over the fence.

Zack's photography skills took on a frenzied dedication. With each step the occurrence of events unraveled.

The car left the road here. Snap. Snap.

Entered the culvert here. Snap. Snap.

Flipped end-over-end until wedged too firmly to move. Snap. Snap. Snap.

He studied the road. A hundred feet ahead was a four-way stop. A one-car accident on dry straight pavement with the longest amount of laid rubber Zack had ever seen. The whole thing didn't add up.

The light tap of a horn made him look up. Chloe drove past. He gave a brief wave. Horror etched across her face made him sorry he'd included her. This promised to be a hard mission. Add to that consoling her. He ground his teeth and found comfort in the stress of his muscles.

Zack studied the smashed car, taking as many photos as he could. As the windows emerged above the concrete, he crouched to spot a driver. The tow truck cut off daylight from the far side and the extra dark tinted windows made it impossible to see inside. He looked up. Cops, standing next to the wench, were peering just as hard from the opposite direction.

He wasn't alone. A uniformed officer, he hadn't

noticed, took a position next to him and squatted, forcing him to rise, while a sports-jacketed cop stood adjacent separated only by the strip of barbed wire fence.

When had they'd crossed to his side of the culvert?

He surveyed the entire scene. Chloe rounded the corner and headed his direction. The car shuddered and a loud scream of metal reclaimed his attention.

The plain-clothes officer spoke. "If your team hadn't won state, you never could have taken Prissy Lambert to the prom."

What?

The cop's profile looked familiar, hazarding a guess he said. "If Old High's quarterback hadn't been a pussy, she wouldn't have gone either."

The uniform officer at his feet snorted. The plain-clothes officer arched an eyebrow. "Pussy? He wasn't the one with a paternity suit slapped against him."

"Neither was I," Zack said, glad for the momentary distraction.

The other man shrugged. "That girl turned out to be a baby making machine. I hear she's got four kids, divorced with another one on the way."

Both men grinned. Thompson hadn't changed that much since high school. Same height, put on a little weight, but it all looked like muscle. Dark hair, dark eyes and a tanned chiseled face. No rounded edges anywhere.

"I'd say we both dodged a bullet," Zack said.

The uniformed officer at their feet gave a low whistle of pure masculine appreciation. Both men turned to follow the direction of his gaze.

Chloe's blonde hair whipped with the gust of breeze. She'd reached up and gathered it into a bundle at her nape. The short sweatshirt rose and showed several inches of flat, firm flesh not covered by her low riding jeans. All the men watched those endless legs wrapped in skin- tight pants as her feet picked a path through the cow pasture. Her golden skin glowed in the early morning sunlight.

"Mine," Zack said.

The cop on the ground tilted his head to look at him. "You're a lucky man."

"Not that lucky." Zack nodded toward the vehicle being jerked out of the concrete. "That's my brother's car."

"I heard you turned down the scholarship from UT to drive for NASCAR."

Zack searched his memory banks to see if he remembered anything about the other man and came up blank. "Yeah, but that only lasted a short while. I ended up in the Navy."

"Bummer."

"Zack's a SEAL." Chloe announced having gotten close enough to hear the last part of the conversation. Both officers looked at Zack with new appreciation.

Chloe reached out a hand to the officer next to Zack. "I'm Chloe La Ruse."

"Detective Thompson Michaels, ma'am."

"Detective, huh?" Zack smiled. To Chloe, he said, "In high school, T-dawg and I competed on rival football teams… for a variety of trophies."

Chloe tilted her head. A quizzical look crossed her features. "What do we know here?"

"Nothing until we get the car out," the detective replied, losing his buddy-buddy charm to his work persona.

"Where's Gordy?" she asked.

"Waiting to see." His words clipped. Professional.

Chloe paled and stepped farther away.

"Let's cross." Thompson gestured toward the concrete ditch. "You knew the driver, ma'am?"

All three men jumped into the culvert. Too late to signal her, she answered before Zack could prevent words he knew would cause the detective's mind to whirl.

"Yes. He was my boyfriend."

Zack groaned silently. Detective Michaels' gaze was on his face and he was careful to hide any hint of his thoughts.

Chloe stood on the ledge, eyeing the drop to hard concrete. Zack held his arms up to lift her. It wouldn't go without notice that he touched her bare skin above her waist. And unless the Detective was blind, Chloe's pleased smile of intimacy said more than words.

"Can you tell me where you were last night?" Detective Michaels asked as he easily leapt up the side.

"Why?" Chloe gave him a blank look.

Zack suppressed a smile. But then her eyes narrowed. She eyed the Detective suspiciously as she fisted her hands on her hips. The fact that she was a foot shorter didn't intimidate her in the slightest. "Detective Michaels, what do you investigate?"

He should have known better, Chloe might have been naïve but she wasn't stupid.

"Homicides."

He couldn't breathe. Every swear word in the English language ran through his mind. Had he not been SEAL trained, they might well have exited his mouth. He'd known in his gut this wasn't an accident. Gordy had been murdered. Zack stood by the ledge unable to force himself up the side.

"Do you need a hand up?" The uniformed officer inquired quietly. Zack shook his head and forced himself to look at Chloe.

Her eyes were wide and her skin was colorless. She blinked several times as he scrambled to be by her side.

"Homicide?" The words sank in. Unshed tears brightened her eyes. "Murder? Where is Gordy?"

"We're about to find out, but in answer to your question. No, I don't think this was a freak one-car accident."

"How can you tell?" she practically whispered.

"The Ferrari was hit from behind. Look at the tire marks. The driver was riding the breaks. There's green paint and a dent on the driver's side." He pointed toward the back tire.

Both Zack and Chloe looked. He pulled out the camera and took a couple of additional shots.

"Riding the brakes?" Chloe asked. "Gordy could've outrun anything on the road. Why wouldn't he have gone faster rather than slow down?"

"When would you have braked?" Detective Michaels asked her.

"For a stop sign?" she questioned, starring at the highway. She shook her head. "A stop sign wouldn't have panicked Gordy. If he thought he was in trouble, he would have blown right through it."

"Of course, anyone with half a brain would." Detective Michaels spoke in a soothing voice.

"But if there were a third, larger vehicle blocking both lanes…" Zack said, picking up the threads of T-dawg's thinking.

"Exactly." He nodded.

"You could tell all that?" Chloe gave him a look of admiration. "You're better than TV detectives."

"Well, thanks, but that isn't exactly the standard we struggle to uphold."

A loud pop and the sound of ripping metal caused everyone to look. The car door peeled away like a lid on a can of tuna. Chloe stepped forward, but Detective Michaels grabbed her arm.

"Stay here."

The officer holding the Jaws of Life signaled to the ambulance driver. Two paramedics wheeled a gurney to the car. One leaned inside the car for several minutes. Then they lifted Gordy's body and placed him on the gurney.

Zack couldn't see anything beyond brief glimpses of Gordy's clothes and a flash of sandy blond hair. And a sheet. They covered his brother's face with a white sheet. His stomach churned. He and death were old friends, but this time it was his younger brother, a boy he should have protected. He struggled to push his reactions down and maintain his demeanor when what he really wanted was to shove the cops aside and pull Gordy to him.

He remembered seeing a woman in Iraq, who clutched her son to her chest and wailed at the heavens. At the time her reaction had disconcerted him, now it seemed like a perfectly normal response.

An officer conferred briefly with the paramedics, nodding while they spoke.

Zack kept his teeth gritted and his countenance blank. Chloe was not as good at hiding her emotions.

Already pale she'd lost all the remaining color in her face.

"Sit," Zack told her quietly. "Before you fall down."

She looked up at him, lost and bewildered. "Gordy's dead," she said, the voice a strangled moan. "How could this happen?" She leaned against him and he offered her support, although he wanted to weep himself. One day late. If he'd just been one day earlier he might have been able to prevent this senseless tragedy.

He closed his eyes, drawing from his reserves. Instead his mind screamed. You have to tell your mother and sister. Tomorrow is Glyn's wedding. He remembered all the excitement last night at the house. His mother and sister would be devastated. Oh Lord, he'd lost his kid brother.

"Zack…" A voice broke into his thoughts and he opened his eyes. Thompson spoke, "I need a statement from both of you before you leave."

Zack nodded and squeezed Chloe closer.

"Detective," an officer called. "You need to see this."

Thompson Michaels walked to the car and looked at whatever the officer held in his hand. The men conferred and the officer pointed his flashlight into the car and gestured with his hand. The Detective directed the flashlight movement. The gloved officer reached into the interior of the car.

In his hand was a large manila envelope. Several of the officers gathered as the envelope was opened.

Michaels looked in Zack's direction. Whatever was in the envelope wasn't good. He said something to his fellow officers, snapped his sunglasses open and pushed them on his nose. His lips pulled into a grim line as he stalked toward them.

"I need detailed statements about where you were yesterday." He grabbed a pen and notebook from his pocket. "And an ID."

Chloe dug out her driver's license and handed it to him. She spoke first. "We were at a class from eleven-thirty till about one-thirty. Zack dropped me off at my apartment. I walked to the grocery store--"

"You walked?"

"My car's on the fritz. Anyway, that was around four. I was home by five-thirty. Then I was in my apartment alone until a little after midnight when Zack got there. I don't have any witnesses. I didn't talk to anyone on the phone. No one can verify where I was." Her voice rose in panic. She tossed her head back and forth as though hunting for an alibi.

Michaels put his hand on her shoulder and gave her a minute to compose herself. "It's okay." He gentled his voice. "For now all we're doing is finding out where everyone was."

She stared at him with wide-eyed disbelief. "I didn't kill him. I didn't even talk to Gordy yesterday."

He nodded, once again trying to be a calming influence. "I believe you. A woman without a car isn't our number one lead."

"How can you believe me?" she snapped, angry that he was dismissing her so easily. "You know nothing about me. I could have rented a car. What if I borrowed one from a friend? I could have been the one who set him up. You don't know this."

Detective Michaels lowered his sunglasses and peered at her over the rims. "You've got an active little imagination, don't you? Judging by your address, I'd say you were a student. Drama or Creative Writing major?"

Chloe's mouth opened in an o. Her shocked expression faded. "Neither. Human Sexuality."

Then it was Detective Michael's turn to stare. Finally, he forced himself to look away, but mumbled, "perfect" under his breath loud enough for Zack to hear. He twisted his lips in an amused look and handed him his military id.

"Let me start with some questions." Detective Michaels said. "Why are you in town? What class were you attending? And where did you go after you left Ms. La Ruse off?"

"My sister's getting married tomorrow. The class was taught by Marlene…"

"Campbell." Chloe answered.

"The sex lady?" Detective Michaels asked, turning his head to look at Chloe again. "Was this the Oriental techniques class?"

Zack refrained from clamping his hands around Chloe's mouth as she elaborated. "No. This was the one on the Kama Sutra."

"Was it good? My girlfriend's hot to register."

That's right, egg her on.

"In many ways it was excellent. She's very detailed, but there is a six-month waiting list. Marlene does a lot of therapeutic work. For example in this group there was a woman who had had two radical mastectomies. And had tattooed her chest with flowers." Chloe demonstrated where the vines began and how they wrapped around her chest.

As Chloe talked a blue streak about Marlene and

the class, Sam looked at Zack helplessly.

He shouldn't feel any sympathy for him, but he did. Leaning over he took the pen from T-dawg's hand and wrote the word BORING on his notepad.

Thompson cleared his throat to hide his chuckle. He raised his hand and signaled another officer. "Officer Williams, give Ms. La Ruse a tour of the outside of the car see if she can remember any damage done prior to this accident."

"There was nothing wrong with the car. Gordy wouldn't even let it get dirty."

Thompson's almost silent groan reached Zack, causing him to smile. "From your research, do you know what a ball gag is?"

She clamped her mouth closed for an entire minute, before finally eking out an answer. "Yes."

"Well, if I hear one more word out of you, I'm going to get one. Go with this officer and keep out of trouble."

Officer Williams grinned, delighted to entertain Ms. La Ruse.

Thompson choked back a laugh. "I'm going to turn my back, so I don't see all the officers making fools of themselves over her. She's a pistol."

"Yeah, but she doesn't know it. Every mirror in her apartment has a hundred notes taped to them with little sayings."

Michaels raised an eyebrow. "Sayings?"

"What are those things called? Affirmations."

A frown furrowed his brow and he shifted to study Chloe again. "Like that guy on Saturday Night Live used to do? The one who looked into the mirror and told himself stuff so he'd feel better."

"Exactly. Oh, and her horoscope."

"That sounds messed up."

Zack shook his head. "Not messed up. Insecure." And charming.

"So whose girlfriend is she?"

Damn, he knew Thompson couldn't wait to ask him that. "She and Gordy went together since high school, but for all intents and purposes they'd broken up. Gordy was sleeping with some waitress at the B&L named Dixie."

Michaels made a note about that. "The class was really boring?" he asked quietly.

Zack shook his head, still unable to believe he's lasted as long as he did. "You wouldn't believe. We left early."

"Where were you last night?"

"Looking for Gordy." Zack detailed the events of the night before.

"You might as well hear it now. The car contained enough crystal meth to put your brother away for twenty to thirty years." Detective Michaels glanced at a piece of paper. "Four empty bottles of beer, two unopened, a receipt showing their purchase yesterday at twelve fifty-seven, and pills scattered everywhere. Somehow I don't think acetaminophen will be the main ingredient. The toxicology report is going to be important, but it'll take weeks to get it back."

Zack forced his head to nod so Michaels would know he heard the words. But all the time his brain was screaming, Gordy. Gordy. How did this happen?

"We've pulled his driving record. No tickets. Could he handle a high-powered vehicle under the influence?"

"He ran Arthur's track yesterday. According to

Arthur, he was high as a kite. The old man threatened him with a lifetime suspension, but it didn't affect his driving. A lot of those runs are recorded. If we catch Arthur early enough today, he might still have it."

Michaels made another note. "I'll go see him. Before you leave I'll need you to identify the body. His seat belt held but he's pretty banged up."

Grimly Zack nodded, then glanced in Chloe's direction. Two Officers were talking to her.

Neither seemed particularly interested in the car. Sam gestured for him to move toward the ambulance.

"Don't let Chloe see." Or his mother. Or his sister. Damn, this was going to ruin Glyn's wedding. But he bet money, Stan, the man wouldn't agree to change the date. Not someone with his degree of predictability.

Chapter Seventeen

"We're on our way there now." Zack assured his sister over the telephone. Chloe closed her eyes and searched for her happy place. "No, it's not good news."

Gordy's dead.

Chloe wanted to scream. She practiced her breathing exercises. Maybe she'd have time to devote an hour to yoga this afternoon. She doubted she could focus enough for meditation.

Zack parked down the street from of his mother's house. Relatives in town for the wedding produced a lot of cars in the driveway and on the street. Chloe's lips were dry. She dug in her purse for gloss, hoping Zack would go in without her.

But Zack was not Gordy. He opened her car door and offered his hand. Together they entered his mother's house with his hand firmly at her back.

Relatives crowded the living room. Chloe attempted to excuse herself as soon as they were in the door to find a place to hide out, but he refused to let her scurry off.

"Zack." Men, she didn't know, patted his back and women kissed him. Several shook her hand and tossed names in her direction. Her head nodded so continuously she feared she'd be mistaken for a bobbled headed doll on someone's dashboard.

Bernice glared at her and whispered to the woman standing next to her. Vaguely, Chloe remembered Bernice's sister, Velda, from a visit several years ago. "Two peas in a pod," Gordy had said.

Zack dragged her to stand next to him in front of the immediate family. It was bad enough she had to deal with her grief, seeing his family's sorrow wouldn't help.

"Gordy's dead," Zack said. Faces stared back in shock and disbelief.

Glynnis burst into tears, which seemed to open the floodgate for others. Stanley wrapped his arm protectively around her. Glyn blew her nose with a loud honking sound that would have made Chloe laugh under different circumstances. For sure, Gordy would have found it hilarious.

"We'll have to cancel the wedding." Glyn said.

"Canceling the wedding won't bring Gordy back." Stanley said. A large vein throbbed in his forehead. "We should go ahead. Everyone's here." When no one objected, he added. "Saturday afternoon we could add a brief memorial service."

"We can't have a wedding and a funeral in the same weekend." Bernice huffed.

"It's not right." Velda seconded.

"No one planned it this way," Zack said. "But the entire family's here. Glyn and Stanley deserve to have their wedding."

Something about the tone of his voice had Chloe searching his face. He spoke the right words, but he wasn't happy about it. Glyn gazed at Stanley who shifted his feet and whispered something in her ear. Her mouth tightened almost imperceptivity. Bernice was not as subtle. Her mouth drew into a line that pinched her upper lip. Temper flamed in her eyes.

"This is her fault," Bernice pointed a finger at Chloe, her lips twisted in a snarl. "If it wasn't for her, my son would be alive."

Gordy's mother had always hated her, she hadn't

realized how much until now. She was getting blamed for Gordy's death? Wait until Detective Michaels heard this. The only thing keeping her from running out the door was Zack's arm still anchored firmly around her waist.

But he was a Pritchard and it wouldn't be long before he blamed her as well. Shit. She had to get out of here.

"Chloe had nothing to do with this," he said. "Casting blame won't help. We need to deal with the logistics of a wedding and a funeral."

Several heads bobbed in agreement. Velda's husband, Uncle Tom asked, "How'd he die?"

# # #

"Murder."

The instantaneous silence and the shocked expressions gave Zack a chance to elaborate further, hoping to change his families' opinion about Chloe's involvement. "Gordy got in with a rough crowd and the police think they killed him." Briefly he described the accident. His mother shook her head in disagreement the entire time he spoke. "Those are the facts, mom."

"Why is she here?" Bernice demanded, pointing once again at Chloe.

Zack felt Chloe automatically step back. This time he let her go and took a step toward his mother. "Because I invited her."

Bernice folded her arms over her chest, refusing to hear his words. "She's not welcome in my house."

"You're over-reacting. Calm yourself. We have problems to solve."

But his mother's anger, once reared, had always

been impossible to contain. "She's always been a bad influence. First, on poor Gordy, and now on you. Are you sleeping with her?"

Wide-eyed aunts and uncles stared at the quickly escalating drama. Zack pushed his anger down and spoke as patiently as his gritted teeth would allow.

"Gordy's been in trouble for a while. The only way he could have afforded that Ferrari was to sell drugs. Deep down inside you and I both knew it."

The room took a collective gasp. All heads bounced between mother and son.

"He only did it for her." Bernice responded. Next to her, Velda nodded.

Zack's temper flared. Why had he not realized how hard this would be on Chloe? "Gordy had some admirable qualities and I loved him, but he was a selfish little prick. He never did a thing he didn't want to do."

Bernice's eyes widened to the point that white could be seen completely around the pupil.

She stamped her foot and rolled her hands into tight fists. Velda's face took on a sly expression as though delighted to see her sister furious.

"Get out of my house. Both of you." Bernice raised her fists. Zack could take a punch, but if that happened they'd never regain control. Maybe it was best to leave and let his family solve the problems however they chose.

Chloe had already reached the door. Other family members stepped aside leaving a path.

Glynnis rose off her chair and headed toward her mother, shaking off Stanley's hand attempting to restrain her. Mediation was never his strong suit. Like his mother, he believed fighting was sometimes the answer. No wonder Gordy was so messed up.

"Well," Velda declared with great satisfaction. "Wes was right. You should've had an abortion."

"What?" Zack stood stock-still. "Who the hell was Wes? What abortion?"

"Wes," Velda said, the delight of her triumph shone in her eyes, "Was your father."

"Hush." Glynnis spoke to her aunt as she put an arm around her mother.

"Arnie was my father."

"No. Bernice was pregnant with you when she met Arnie. Wes ran out on her. Told her to have an abortion and left." She announced with a flourish of her arm.

"Velda, shut up," Uncle Tom said.

Zack looked at his mother and sister before searching the faces scattered around the room. There were a few surprised looks, but for the most part it was mainly embarrassment. Everyone knew -- but him.

He didn't react. He couldn't. Processing one more shocking bit of personal information was too hard for him to handle. He'd think about it later. His family could go to Hell for all he cared.

"Let's go," he said to Chloe.

Zack refused to speak as he drove. Chloe chewed on her thumbnail. When they reached her apartment, he stopped the car. "Can you download the pictures we took today?"

She nodded.

"I'm going to find Thompson Michaels and see if he can tell me anything more."

Chloe awkwardly struggled out of the car, her face a mask of numbness, and her eyes dull. Zack put the car in reverse. When he left Riggers this time, he'd never come back. There'd be no reason. Glynnis would be happily married.

And he wasn't flawed enough for his mother to love him.

Chapter Eighteen

"There's nothing more I can tell you. We are investigating all the leads, but you've got to back off and let us do our job," Thompson said, while Zack leaned against a wooden counter at the police station. The desk sergeant buried his head in his paperwork, but Zack didn't doubt for a minute he savored every word.

"We did get the tapes from Arthur and they confirm that Gordy was in control of the car even under the influence. I'm sorry."

Zack walked out of the police station more frustrated than ever. There was nothing for him to do here. He should leap on a plane and head back to California.

Chloe's cell phone rang. He'd forgotten he still had it with him. He glanced at the Caller ID. Glyn.

"You still planning on giving me away?"

"If you'll have me."

"Oh, Zack, I'm so sorry about this afternoon. You know how mother gets. And Velda's just like her. They were unbelievably awful to you."

"And to Chloe," he said to gage her reaction.

"I guess."

"You believe she's responsible for all Gordy's problems?"

"No, of course, not. But I don't understand why you are staying with her. It looks bad and has the family on edge."

Zack sighed. Chloe had no defenders in his family. "She's a friend."

"The rehearsal dinner's tonight at six o'clock."

Glyn paused, then added. "Zack, for my sake, please don't bring her. It'll just create problems."

"For your sake, I won't," he agreed, wondering how he would tell Chloe. This is why the Navy was perfect. One didn't have to get involved.

Guilt carried him as far as stopping by the store for things he thought Chloe might need. He purchased tissues, chicken noodle soup, a couple of small containers of expensive chocolate ice cream and tea.

In his mind he practiced excuses for why he wasn't taking her with him. She might not want to go anyway, since the whole family blamed her for Gordy's death. He mounted the steps to her apartment. A hot pink sticky note clung to her door.

"Be back later."

Short and to the point, but no information. Once inside, he shook his head as he eyed the changes that had taken place in the living room in the two hours he'd been gone. She either watched way too much TV or had the mind of a criminal investigator. A white board was set up with photos and a hand-drawn diagram of the accident.

A flip chart had questions written in color-coded markers.

Who killed Gordy? Why? Questions about the murder were in red.

How long had he been selling meth? For whom? Drugs rated dark brown.

How did he spend his last twenty-four hours? Who are his friends? Who are his enemies? Gordy's personal issues were detailed in navy blue.

Was there money involved? Where did he sell the drugs? To whom? Why did he need to die? Anger? Revenge? Did Gordy cheat someone? Did he have other drugs besides those on him?

Followed by a bulleted list of ideas in hot pink.

Check Gordy's cell phone. Check his bank accounts. If he didn't put money in the bank, where would it be?

Stacks of papers sat next to her computer. She'd been busy. The Internet had provided her with a wealth of documents: crime scene investigation, methamphetamines, dockets of upcoming court cases, and physics zones: forces, acceleration and car accidents.

Zack stood open-mouthed for several minutes. Chloe felt exactly the same way he did, but unlike him, she was actually doing something about it. She was eliminating possibilities and considering answers.

Had he misjudged her? He'd spent hours fantasizing about her, but never once considered there might be more to her than a gorgeous face and a killer body.

Zack re-read her notes, again begging the main question where-to-start? And the answer to that very question opened the door behind him.

Chloe stepped into the apartment holding a large box in her hands. A cabdriver entered behind her with another equally large box. Zack stepped forward to help her, but before he could help, she dropped the box.

She pointed next to the box she'd just deposited. "Just put it here, Phil."

"What's all this?" Zack asked while mentally questioning his status in her life.

Chloe didn't answer. Instead she reached into her purse and tipped the cabdriver. "Thanks. I'll call you if I need you."

"Any time." The fifty-something cab driver looked Zack over, sizing him up, man-to-man. "You'll be okay?" he asked Chloe.

Zack refrained from snarling to get him to leave.

"I'll be fine," she assured the man as she ushered him out the door. "He's a friend."

A friend? Zack wanted to protest, but let it drop. After all, he'd said the same thing about her earlier.

"What's in the boxes?" He bent over opening the one nearest to him.

"Papers from Gordy's house. I went through everything and gathered up as much as I could."

Zack straightened, took her arm. He didn't want her running away. He needed answers. "The police let you do that?"

"They weren't there." She pulled against his hand to free her arm. "It was obvious they hadn't been there, either."

"You have a key?"

She shrugged. "I have a shoe that went through the back window."

Next he'd been bailing her out of jail.

"Okay, Mata Hari, before you get arrested for breaking and entering, I'll teach you some lock-picking tricks."

She tossed her hair, affected disinterest, but her eyes sparkled. She wanted to know. "Like the one you used to get past the dead bolt last night?"

"Yeah." Zack grinned. "Now, what are you looking for in all of this?"

"Financial records, notes, phone numbers -- something to give us an idea of Gordy's life." She dropped to her knees and scooped up a handful of papers, then plopped down on the floor and sorted the papers into stacks. "Like -- who was his new girlfriend? I found a tube of cheap lipstick and a tacky black bra under his bed."

Another conversation he was dying to have.

"A girl named Dixie, a waitress at the B&L. Was the bra… um… large?"

Chloe raised her head. Surprise written across her face. "You knew about this?"

"…Uh… I… uh…"

Her lips drew into a pucker. He could see how she had perfected her skills as a teacher.

"Don't lie to me." She shook her head, dismissing him. "Never mind."

Zack fumbled. "She's not as pretty as you are."

Chloe rolled her eyes. "Zack, the bra had peek-a-boo nipples and the lipstick was the most ghastly shape of plum. Believe me I don't need your help to picture her." Chloe dropped her head and returned to her sorting.

What did she hope to accomplish? "Why are you doing this?"

"I'm a graduate student. Research is what I do. If you want to help, let's organize all this stuff."

Paperwork? She thought Gordy left a note? By the way, if I'm killed, so-and-so will be the murderer. Was she crazy? "What will this tell us?"

Chloe raised her head at his tone. "His life. Everyone's life is a paper trail."

Zack disagreed. Not everyone's. He knew the extent the Navy's Intel went to ensure his life wasn't a paper trail. But he was the exception, not the rule. She was right. People did leave paper trails. "When this is over, I want to read your thesis."

Chloe raised her eyes from the sorting; a slow

blush crossed her cheeks. "You do?" She smiled shyly. "No one's asked to read it except the faculty advisors."

"I can tell by the way your mind works that it's going to be good. Is it close to finished?"

Had her major been anything but human sexuality he would have asked about the topic. What if she studied something bizarre? Like bondage? He'd never needed to tie a woman up. He understood some of what Gordy had felt.

"Soon," she said, but her attention was already elsewhere as she studied each scrap of paper and dropped it into one stack or another.

Chapter Nineteen

The evening of the rehearsal dinner, Stanley greeted Zack in the corridor of the restaurant. Behind him in the private dining room, Zack saw a flurry of activity. His mother, sister and a half-dozen other women were putting the final touches on the room.

"Where's Chloe?" Stanley shook his hand. He'd never disliked Stanley. In some ways they were alike. Both had chosen positions of protection, but each man saw danger from a different point of view. Still he'd never gotten a feel for the man's character.

"Glyn asked me not to bring her for the sake of family harmony."

Stanley frowned slightly, turned his head and sought out Glyn in the crowd. "Not everyone believes Gordy was an innocent misled by a beautiful woman."

Although Stanley's support pleased him, he didn't have an appropriate comment to make. He settled for "thanks."

For the first time, he wondered if he might actually like Stanley someday.

Stanley opened his mouth to say something more when Bernice shrieked. Both men looked, but it was Stanley who muttered, "Now what?"

Bernice waved her hand over the table. As usual, something was not to her liking. Another woman tried to calm her.

"I'll see if I can help Mom," Stanley said.

Only one other woman stood next to Bernice. Stanley's mom. Zack had nothing else to do, but stay out of the way, so he followed him into the room.

"What's the problem?" Stanley asked as they approached the table.

"Bernice feels," the woman said, twisting her hands nervously. "We should have done complete place settings rather than letting people sit where they want. I thought the head table would be enough." Her worried expression belied the soft tone of her voice.

Glynnis chewed her lip as she stood behind their mother. When she had become so cowered? As a child she hadn't been that way. Of course, he didn't remember his mother being so unforgiving and rigid either.

Stanley straightened. "Bernice, things are as they are. Glyn and I agreed a seating chart isn't necessary for this small a group."

Bernice whirled to face her daughter. Glyn looked pale as she rubbed her temples like she had a doozy of a headache.

"Maybe," Glyn's voice was flat. "We could hurry and get one done."

"Could I talk to you outside?" Stanley cupped her elbow and tried to steer her toward the exit. Glyn refused to budge.

"No time. We can draw up a plan and write out place cards in a few minutes. I'm sure the restaurant has something we can use." Glyn pivoted her head between her mother and her future husband.

"NOW." Stanley snarled. Zack's fist curled, but he restrained himself.

Glynnis looked at Stanley as though seeing him for the first time. "All right."

Zack twisted his neck to relieve his tension. He couldn't believe that Glyn had grown into such a meek woman. She certainly hadn't been that as a child.

"Well," Bernice huffed. "This is inexcusable."

"Mother, when did you get such a big stick up your butt?" Zack asked, irritated with her attitude and antics. A gruff snort came from Stanley as he and Glyn stepped out the side door.

"Zachary Tyler Pritchard. Things need to be done appropriately."

He restrained himself from rolling his eyes, knowing it would irritate her further.

"Since the Queen isn't coming, perhaps you can give the rules a little slack and aim for a pleasant evening."

As rehearsal dinners went, it was one of the least joyous occasions he could remember. Nobody was happy. Grief was another presence in the room, with the empty chair next to Bernice a constant reminder of their loss.

Glyn appeared jumpy and tense. Stanley scowled each time he was addressed. Zack watched Glyn's face and tried to decide if her bright eyes were the result of happiness or tears. He leaned toward the latter.

Several members of his family made a point of speaking to him, while others gave him a wide berth. He counted the minutes until he could slip out. Bernice sat at a table near the bride and groom while Zack chose the furthest seat he could manage from hers.

Thank God, Chloe wasn't here, even though seeing his family was such a mess wouldn't come as a surprise to her. Guests arrived slowly. Zack's table was still empty when the waiters brought the salad.

"I can move you to another table, if you'd

prefer," the hostess said.

He was tempted to ask if she would put him in another restaurant, but refrained. He nodded and rose to be relocated. The restaurant door opened and a man and two women entered.

"Oh, good. Late arrivals," the hostess said with forced cheer. She raised her hand and the man spotted her and led the party his direction. Zack retook his seat.

The man sat beside Zack and the two women beyond him. He introduced himself as Bruce Porter. All worked for OHSA.

"You work with Stanley?"

Bruce chuckled. "Actually, no. Stanley works in emissions analysis. We do field inspections."

"Ah," He said, stymied for another reaction.

"Actually," the woman leaned around Bruce to add, "We were kind of surprised to be invited to the rehearsal dinner since we're not related or in the wedding party."

Zack nodded, but Bruce confided in a voice low enough not to be overheard. "Stanley dated Fran," he nodded his head in the direction of the other, younger woman. Brown hair, brown eyes, not unattractive, but not pretty either. A lot like his sister.

"How long ago?"

"Right up until he announced he was marrying another woman. It took us all by surprise. Fran got the impression that he and Glyn were polygamous."

Zack hid his surprise. Was Glyn into multiple partners? He looked up to find Stanley watching their table intently.

"Was he inviting Fran to join them?"

Bruce turned his head to speak into Zack's ear. "Well, at least him."

By seven-thirty, dinner had been cleared. Stanley's father struggled out of his wheelchair and stood to give a toast. Zack groaned inwardly. Would he be expected to give a toast? Probably. It wasn't that he didn't know any toasts. His Naval companions had provided him with a multitude over the years, but none appropriate for his sister's wedding.

Before his father rose completely, Stanley spoke, "We'd like to wait until dessert is served before the toasting."

Stanley's father faltered but sat back down. Neither Glyn nor Stanley smiled.

Waiters carried flaming baked Alaskas into the room, one after another. Everyone applauded and for the first time smiles broke out. The tension in the room receded for a moment.

Zack understood it was difficult to project joy on the same day Gordy was killed, but he thought the bride and groom should have been struggling to hide their happiness, instead of looking like the poster children for misery.

When the waiters left, Stanley and Glyn rose to their feet. Tepid clapping broke the silence and several raised a glass in their direction. Stanley held up his hand and waited patiently for the room to settle.

The couple stood stiffly, but held hands, occasionally murmuring to the other. Someone poured more wine for the couple even as Stanley waved them off.

"We would like to thank everyone for coming. We know many of you have traveled great distances to be with us." His face somber, his eyes on Glynnis.

"A wedding is a time of great celebration and happiness, but with the death of Glyn's brother this morning, we feel…" Stanley's voice cracked.

His sister wrapped her arm around his waist and continued, "This is not our time. We've agreed to postpone our wedding date to a happier time."

The couple kissed. Their lips almost missing as light as the kiss appeared. "We are still very much in love." Stanley's eyes filled with tears. Glynnis stroked his cheek.

Turning to the group, she said, "But we don't want to start our life under the cloud of Gordy's death."

Zack felt like he'd taken a blow to the chest as sorrow welled within him. The chattering of the guests escalated around him. First Gordy. Now Glynnis. What were they thinking?

Granted, marrying into the Pritchard family was no bargain, but in three years, Stan-the-man should have known what it was like.

As the noise diminished, the groom called for attention again. "We have one last announcement to make. Glynnis has been offered a position in the cardiac ward at MD Anderson in Houston, a job she intends to take at the end of next week."

Glyn couldn't take it anymore? This didn't sound like a last minute decision. They weren't postponing the wedding because of Gordy. They were calling it off.

Bernice jumped to her feet. "You can't leave. I'll be alone without you and Gordy." His mother's face was not sad, nor was there fear. Instead he saw a woman who had dominated and bullied her daughter for years and was sure to continue.

A sad smile curved Glyn's lips. "You'll get along

fine, mother. You always have."

Glynnis declared her independence not only from her mother but from her inflexible fiancé as well. Why did "way to go" feel like the wrong thing to say?

Chapter Twenty

Chloe sat cross-legged on the floor of the living room sorting Gordy's papers. The task occupied only a small portion of her attention. The wedding had taken her mind off her continuous worry about her thesis. But tonight Zack had reminded her that her thesis was due soon.

The closer she got to finishing the paper; the further it was from complete. One final interview lingered. For weeks the idea languished in the back of her mind.

Gordy's death, useless as it'd been, was helpful in one unexpected way. For the first time the lack of symmetry in her life took center stage. The vague gap she'd successfully ignored now demanded a solution.

She'd crisscrossed the State of Texas for the past eighteen months interviewing exotic dancers. Except for the most important one. Chloe needed to meet her mother.

Other dancers had children. Most, despite the myth, were not working their way through school on their way to becoming lawyers and doctors and social workers. The lure of money seduced many into the profession and held them there long after the honeymoon period ended.

Like choosing a career in sports, every one of the women she interviewed understood dancing was a young woman's career and a temporary gig at best. Some performers became astute business managers investing in real estate and the stock market, using strategic planning.

While others lived for the day, spending the loot faster than it came in her garters. Sooner or later that life came to an end.

Why then was her mother at forty-two still working the Strip in Vegas? Plus there were the personal questions, the ones she never allowed herself to consider.

Would her mother like her? Approve of her life and who she was becoming? Would she like Zack?

Zack? Zack? He wasn't a permanent fixture in her life. As soon as his sister was married, he would jump on a plane and be gone, never to return. Thanks in part to Gordy's death and Velda's mean little announcement.

That was okay. Chloe had known the rules. She wasn't sorry she'd slept with him. She really wasn't. He'd been a learning experience. Just like being excluded from the rehearsal dinner and the wedding hadn't mattered.

No way would she would have gone.

I am completely filled with the joy and light of the world.

One day a man would come along who was meant to be hers. Someone -- just not Zack.

Chloe sighed and buried her head in her hands. If she had a long dress, she could dance around a lake singing lyrics, like 'someday my prince will come' while animated birds chirped around her head.

Optimism sucked.

# # #

Zack rarely drank beyond an occasional beer. Over the years he'd made plenty of stupid decisions, but the ones he regretted had usually been alcohol induced.

"You're driving me to drink, Bernice," was a

phrase Arnie used with his mother when they'd argued. After today Zack truly understood his father's feelings. But it wasn't limited to his mother. His entire family acted like the pit crew for the Jim Beam 500.

Riggers, Texas had been the one safe haven, protecting his family and offering him sanctuary when the world came on too strong. He was left anchorless. Now all he was doing was swabbing the blood off the deck. More and more the Navy refused to let him participate in field exercises, insisting he was too valuable to be in the field. His job was to train and monitor his team from afar. Plenty of outside opportunities were available, but so far none had made Zack jump ship. Other SEALs had found happiness on the outside. Surely, he could, too.

Home was adrift. His job was disappearing and he was left floundering for a rock to anchor his life.

As his relatives subdued by his sister's announcement filed to their cars, he headed for the restaurant bar. Barely seated he ordered a double scotch on the rocks and drummed his fingers while he checked out the quiet room.

When the bartender delivered the drink, Zack raised the glass and offered a mock toast.

"There once was a girl from Nantucket…"

The bartender chuckled, then nodded at someone over Zack's shoulder. He didn't turn, preferring to put the cold glass to his lips and belt down a large enough swallow he could feel the burn.

"I've always heard it was a man from Nantucket," Thompson said, sliding into the barstool next to his.

"I know that one, too. When you've been in the Navy long enough, you've even heard about dogs from Nantucket."

"Nantucket's a busy town."

"Apparently."

"How's your family holding up?"

Zack raised his eyebrows and shook his head. How could he tell Thompson his family had fallen into the abyss of insanity?

T-dawg accepted his answer. "You thinking about leaving?"

"Don't know." He took a long swallow, draining his glass. Then stared at the ice cubes and debated ordering another before deciding against it. "You like being a cop?"

Thompson shrugged. "Some days," he admitted. "Other days I'm not so sure."

Zack understood. When his team spent too much time in California, he felt the same. He wanted to be active, busy, on the go. Not waiting.

"You're not under suspicion and I'm not legally holding you. But I'd appreciate it if you could give me as much time as possible."

Zack looked at the man sitting next to him. Tough. Competent, but compared to the men on his SEAL team, soft. Cops weren't warriors. Their end was not to take the tango's down, it was to get the drug dealers to court. Not the same thing at all. T-dawg wanted his help, but only to a point.

"Turnabout is fair play. How'd you know it wasn't a one car accident?"

"I told you this morning."

Zack harrumphed. "Liar. That car flipped end-over-end. The things you pointed out this morning were a result of careful study not instant observation.

You've seen an accident like this before."

Thompson rose to leave. "Yeah, but I'd deny it if anyone asks."

"The green paint's your best lead," Zack said, joining him. "Do you have an idea on the vehicle that did it?"

"A real strong one. But we're not looking to take down one player. We want the whole setup."

Zack nodded, pleased by his words. That's the way he would have handled it, too.

"To do that we may need your help."

"You got it." He shook his head and wondered if the cop had any clue what a SEAL could do.

Chapter Twenty One

Zack could hardly wait to get to the relative comfort of Chloe's apartment, but specifically her welcoming arms and warm bed. Even from the parking lot he could see every window in her apartment lit up as he pulled into the last empty spot.

Nice. She'd waited up for him. As he opened the door her surprised expression told him maybe he'd misread the situation. Chloe sat in the middle of the floor surrounded by scraps of paper, her laptop open on the coffee table next to her. As quickly as he'd ever seen her move she snatched the wire rimmed glasses off her nose and stuck them behind her back.

"What are you doing?" he asked, hiding his amusement at her vanity. Last night she'd worn the sexy nightgown. Tonight she was all business. The two braids on either side of her head lowered her age while the glasses raised her IQ. The well-worn flannel bathrobe with the prissy little floral print and leopard-print fleece socks screamed hands-off.

"You're too quiet. I didn't hear you come up the stairs." The cool tones of her voice re-enforced the message of her outfit. Tonight didn't include sex.

"Would you prefer I knocked?" he asked, toeing off his shoes. He dropped his lightweight sports coat to the couch and loosened the tie. He hadn't wore a tie since joining the Navy, but he saved his dress uniform for the wedding. Looks like that wouldn't be needed.

Chloe's eyes narrowed. She wanted to be angry. He suspected it wasn't over the quietness of his steps. "You know women who wear glasses turn me on."

He almost laughed as she worked hard to look annoyed and keep the smile from her lips. "As opposed to women who don't wear glasses who also turn you on."

Is that what she thought? That he was easy?

"I'm pickier than you think. Tell me what you're working on." He changed the subject, refusing to get into an exchange of sexual histories.

"Gordy's expenses. I've done a spreadsheet on his bank account and gone through his phone bills."

He settled on the floor beside her. "What've you found?"

Chloe pointed to the flip chart against the wall. On it was written three local phone numbers.

"He called these three phone numbers regularly. Who are they? His bank account," she said, holding up a stack of papers, "Was kept to a minimum with only enough money to pay rent and utilities which means he probably has a slew of cash around somewhere and maybe more drugs."

She studied the spreadsheet and grimaced. Without saying a word, she placed her glasses on her nose and read from her computer. "Everything else he paid with cash. Aside from the car, he spent a bundle on clothes. The rest is insignificant. I have an errand to run in the morning, why don't I drop you off at Gordy's house and let you search?"

Zack couldn't believe how adorable she looked. He leaned back against the couch and ran a hand through his hair as he considered her proposal. "What errand?"

She stood up and studied the accident chart on the white board. "Oh, nothing important. What time do the police think the accident happened?"

"Why?"

"Because we got called slightly after five this morning. That road is fairly busy and even though the car was in the culvert, the bright yellow color and the tail end in the air would have been seen at night by a passing motorist."

"True. Which means the accident happened between four and five this morning or someone would have seen it."

Zack followed her reasoning. "Who owns this land?" He pointed to land on either side of the highway.

"I don't know. Tomorrow's Friday. I can look at Courthouse records after my errand."

"I'm going to grab a shower. Then let's hit the sack."

"Go ahead, I want to finish here before I join you."

"By the way, Glyn and Stanley called off the wedding."

"You're kidding." Chloe said, but her attention had already left the conversation as she stared at the white board.

Zack stretched out on the bed to wait for Chloe. He shut his eyes prepared to wake up when she crawled into bed. Two hours later he opened his eyes to a still empty bed.

Chloe lay asleep on the living room couch. Her glasses perched on her nose. An Internet printout scattered on the floor. Scooping her off the couch, he tucked her in bed next to him. A robe, a nightgown, socks. Way too many clothes. She needed to be comfortable.

# # #

At five a.m. Chloe's eyes flew open. Damn, she hated that. Today of all days she could've used a little more sleep.

"Don't even think about getting up. Yesterday morning I let you leave. Not today." Zack's husky voice whispered in her ear.

Considering the only muscles she'd moved were her eyelids she was surprised he knew she was awake.

And naked.

How handy was that?

Chapter Twenty Two

Spooned against her back, Chloe felt Zack's hard body. The crinkly hairs on his thighs tickled. She didn't squirm. Any movement she made would be taken as an invitation by the rock-hard erection pressed against her buttocks. His large hand drifted from her waist to the bare breasts above it.

"No sex," she said, pleased by the firmness in her voice.

He nuzzled her neck. "Why?"

"You're leaving."

He gently pinched her nipple. "Not for a while."

Every nerve in her body went on red-alert. Her hand moved to capture his and stop his questing fingers. "Soon."

"Thompson Michaels asked me to stay longer."

Now they were both holding her breast while he kissed her neck. His teeth nibbled on her earlobe and her body came alive.

Concentrating on their conversation, she asked, "He did? When?"

"Last night. Roll over."

Chloe rolled over, but not because he asked. "Was I the only person in the world not invited to the rehearsal dinner?"

Oops. She hadn't meant to say that aloud.

Zack grinned. "Thompson wasn't invited. He caught up with me afterwards. Believe me, you should be glad you didn't go."

"That doesn't make me happy," she said, giving vent to her hurt feelings.

He loomed over the top of her. "Poor baby, let

me make you feel better."

Her next words were swallowed as his mouth came down on hers. The man could kiss. Man, could he kiss. And kiss he did.

She tried to hold back, to maintain some degree of control. She failed. The fierceness with which their tongues tangled had her needs spiraling. Any protests she'd considered traveled through her brain and out her ear, down the side of the bed and puddled on the cheap carpeting.

Ruthlessly he captured her awareness. Repressed desire and longing ignited a blaze of punishing wantonness. She clutched him, arched up to him, and demanded he take what she gave.

Hot, wild, unchecked. Passion poured through her, deafening her to all sound but the roaring in her ears. Mounting flames burned between her legs.

His lips trailed a path to her naked breasts already hard with wanting. At the touch of his heated breath on her nipple, she gave into passion and went still.

Her ragged breathing indicated the extent of her arousal. He took her nipple into his mouth, his tongue brushing gently until the peak was wet and tender.

Though out he'd whispered reassurances, but the words were meaningless and she responded with incoherent murmurings, her brain unable to form words.

The prickle of his beard tickled her skin as his kisses followed his hands toward her navel. Hot breath on the cool damp path caused her to quiver.

Her legs parted easily at his touch. Her head, flung back against the pillows, raised slightly as a low moan escaped her lips. Widening the angle between her thighs, he slipped his fingers downward, pressing against her moist heated flesh.

The sight of his almost black hair buried between her pale thighs excited her. The slightest breath electrified and amplified her already over-heated body. The coolness of his tongue failed to squelch her burning need. Instead the delicate stabbing and gentle probing enflamed her.

She arched. He rose upward, snagged a pillow, and forced it beneath her back for support. Drawing her knees upward, he devour her with his lips and questing tongue.

Chloe moaned, unable to restrain even the slightest whimper. Her voice rose in tempo to the impending volcanic reaction that lurked just beyond her reach. Just as she felt the frustration of failure, Zack ignited the explosion by inserting a finger inside her. Then two.

Chloe was so ensconced in the throes of her orgasm he could've added a tribe of torch-bearing pygmies and she wouldn't have noticed.

# # #

Her responsiveness thrilled him. Briefly his mind envisioned this sizzling sex in the controlled atmosphere of the classroom and grinned. With a condom in place he pressed against her, hesitant to try different positions until her body accustomed itself to his size. Hot, wet and eager she was ready for him.

Her eyes flickered open. Her tight fit had him holding back until he saw the green light of her sated smile. Diving into her was heaven. A velvet sheath made especially for him.

The warm, spicy aroma of arousal surrounded them and heightened his enjoyment of her perfect body. Her breasts jiggled, waving at him, taunting him, but he couldn't stop now. Her legs wrapped around his back spurred him forward. She held the reins and drove him hard, urging him with her breathy crooning sounds.

"Zack." His name was whispered on the wind as she shattered beneath him. It was the sweetest sound he'd ever heard. Unable to hold back, his heart and body followed.

He lay on top of her, struggling to regain his breath. His sanity was already gone. Ratcheting himself up he wanted to draw out of her before she saw how shaken he was.

Over an orgasm.

The most explosive orgasm he'd ever experienced. This was twice she'd affected him this way. Over sex. Simple sex. Except it wasn't simple. It was explosive, mind numbing, life changing sex.

"Not yet," she mumbled, reaching to hold him tighter. "It feels too good to move."

Not for him. He needed to put some distance between them. He couldn't fall in love with Chloe. He was a SEAL. When duty called, SEALs left. Sometimes they never returned.

Over the years teammates had married, but it'd had never worked. Those guys either quit at their wife's insistence or they got a divorce. He hated the obligatory family calls he was forced to attend when a guy didn't make it. Putting on his dress uniform or ice cream suit as it was known, shuffling his feet and murmuring his sympathies didn't bring back a husband or a daddy.

He wasn't superstitious. Unlike Chloe he didn't have hex-warding quotes taped to his mirror. However, he understood protection rituals. Every man on his team wanted to come home when a mission finished, but in order to survive each was prepared to risk everything including death to make it happen. Adding a wife and kids to that mix never worked.

This thing with Chloe was just sex. Great sex, but only sex. Falling in love with a woman who lived across the country wasn't possible.

Next semester she'd be in Indiana and for the little time he was states-side, he'd be in California or Virginia. Hell, next week he'd be home and she'd still be here. Then what? His focus would be on terrorists. Not a pretty little blonde, he'd left behind. At least if he wanted to succeed it better not be. His men counted on him for one-hundred-ten percent.

Zack eased out of her arms and headed into the bathroom to think. Staring in the mirror, he tried to rationalize his behavior. Chloe was one hot chick.

He hung his head over the sink, closed his eyes and knew the truth. He loved Chloe La Ruse in a forever kind of way.

Chapter Twenty Three

Chloe adjusted the seat in the rental car. Zack's long legs required the seat set in the furthest position, she could touch the petals but it was a reach.

A thrill of excitement ran through her as she waved goodbye and waited until he'd entered his brother's house before she flipped open the small notebook. Zack hadn't pressed and she hadn't told him what she planned to do.

She'd been a student for seventeen years. This was the first time she'd ventured outside the box. Gordy's notebook was filled with figures. Chloe suspected the numbers had to be pricing, but since she didn't understand the quantities, she wasn't sure exactly what they signified.

However, she completely understood the schedule outlined on the back few pages. Gordy could be found at certain parking lots on specific days of the week. At first she assumed that was where he made contacts for the drug sales.

Her original plan had been to drive through each parking lot until she saw a pattern. That would work fine as long as Zack was in town and she could use his car, but sooner or later she needed another idea that didn't involve a vehicle.

The last page of the notebook solved her problem - a simple three-line memo.

J Nors
M-S
11-1

Somebody ate lunch every day at Junior's BBQ.

Even an idiot could figure this out. But it also told her other things. Gordy wasn't in all those parking lots, his contact was. Gordy hated barbeque, but even if he had loved it, eating lunch at the same place day would have offended his sense of cool.

The sun was shining, but not too hot. Her blood zinged as she parked the car under a pecan tree on a run-down edge of the downtown business district. At the end of the cul-de-sac, she spotted the telltale sign, tilted over the road. Technically there was an open space under the sign, but no one ever parked there.

Not only was Riggers an oil-boom town, but was located smack-dab in the center of tornado alley. About every ten years, a whopper of a storm came through and made the resident's question why they lived here.

One of the evidences of the storm was a heavy kidney-shaped sign affixed to a steel post that over the years had moved from upright to tilt at least a forty-five degree angle. Every heavy windstorm the locals placed bets on the signs' longevity. According to rumor it had survived fifty years in that position. Slowly the betting had changed. The smart money backed the theory that after the apocalypse, cockroaches would survive and the sign would still hang suspended in peril.

Junior's seedy little tucked-away dump was hardly a tourist destination despite boasting the best BBQ in north Texas. The sign was the least of its problems.

Junior's BBQ
Established 1948

Flashing neon lights in faded pink and green worked as well as could be expected in a building that hadn't seen any renovations since its original construction. At night when the painted letters couldn't be read, the missing neon letters read:

J n or s BQ

Locals in the know simply referred to the BBQ joint as J Nors. Gordy was in the know.

For a popular hangout it was small. The white stucco construction with few windows and a dark paneled interior had limited seating. The dim interior boasted only ten tables and hid a health standard that many suspected fell below normal. Rarely was all the seating taken. What kept the place in business was the superior barbeque and curbside service.

Waitresses didn't last long. It was reputed to be hard work, low tips and long hours. Chloe was pretty sure the help-wanted sign had also been in the window since its inception in 1948.

Dressed in jeans and a tidy t-shirt, the uniform of the waitress, Chloe approached the building. A resume would be superfluous.

The screen door banged announcing her presence. At nine-thirty in the morning, the restaurant was empty. But the noise from the kitchen told her where the action was.

Small, cramped and cluttered, the kitchen scarcely had room for the three employees yelling at each other. She expected to see anger, but realized the screaming was necessary to be heard over the noisy vent-a-hood, running water and banging pans.

From the doorway Chloe tried to determine who was in charge. A large white man with a sauce-stained apron standing front of the ovens or a small wizen black woman rolling out dough at a butcher-block table. She eliminated the youngest of the three, a middle-age Mexican man carrying a vat of potato salad from the walk-in.

All saw her at the same time.

The chubby oven guy leaned around the pot rack and checked her out from head to toe. "What do you want?"

"To apply for a job."

The work came to a dead-halt and all three looked her over. The black woman snorted and returned to her pastry, but the two men continued to stare.

"Back or front?"

"What?"

"Front," the three said unison.

"You want to be a waitress?" the white guy asked.

"Yeah."

He tilted his head to see the clock. "Gertie will be here in a few minutes. Grab a seat in the dining room. Help yourself to a beer if you want one."

"No, thanks."

Chloe sat in the dining room and listened to the three discuss her. She couldn't decide if they didn't think she could hear them or didn't care. Basically their summary was too cute, too classy, too inexperienced. No way would Gertie hire her.

Another door slammed.

"Damnation. Georgia called in sick. How the hell

are we going to get through lunch?" A gravelly older female voice asked. Without seeing her face, Chloe had her pegged for a three-pack-a-day smoker.

"A girl out-front wants a job. No experience."

"Well slap my butt and call me happy. My problems solved themselves."

"REALLY inexperienced." A male voice cautioned.

"If she can stand and breathe, she's in."

Loud laughter followed and the kitchen door swung open to reveal a short, squat woman who looked like she wrestled pit bulls for fun. Chloe had a momentary twinge of sympathy for the dogs.

"That's right, God. Make a mockery of my problems." She announced to the ceiling. To Chloe, she said, "Honey, have you ever done a hard day's work?"

"Sure."

"If I wasn't in the weeds, you'd be out on your ear, but I need you. You're here, so I assume you're just as desperate." She sighed. "Stand up. Let's get a look at you."

Chloe stood. The short woman circled her making tsking noises with her tongue. "Well, you'll liven up the place. But let me tell you, if I had your face, I'd be turning tricks before I'd wait tables in this dump."

What did one say to that?

"Here," Gertie tossed an apron at her. "You and I'll work together until things start hoppin'. Then you'll be on your own. I'll make sure the clowns in the kitchen don't give you any problems."

Outfitted with an apron, an order pad and a pen, Gertie walked Chloe through the basic details. A bartender arrived a few minutes after ten.

"We're like McDonalds, honey. We don't change our menu. People know what they want. Prices are posted on the wall outside and next to the cash register. I'll ring everything up. Just leave the money here." She gestured toward a narrow ledge next to the register.

"Must be eleven o'clock. Bubba just pulled in. Give me a red draw."

The bartender mixed the beer and tomato juice in an icy mug and shoved it across the counter to Gertie.

"Bubba's a regular and a real nice guy. He's a little peculiar, but waitin' on him is a snap."

Chloe followed Gertie out the door. Bubba drove a beat up dark blue Chevy pickup. He didn't park under the awning but at the back of the lot designated for overflow parking.

"How come he parks back here?" Chloe asked as they hiked up an incline. Gertie didn't answer.

"Hey," she yelled.

"Hey, yourself." Bubba called back. "New girl?"

The heavy bald man hung out the window and sized her up. The hair on her arm's rose, but she forced herself to keep moving following in Gertie's footsteps.

"Yeah, first day. This here's Chloe." Gertie attached the tray to Bubba's window and took the frosted mug from Chloe. From her apron pocket she dug out a saltshaker and placed it on the tray.

"Pretty name." he said as he emptied enough salt in the beer to make it foam. The man was going to have a heart attack. No one looked alarmed.

"Where's the green truck?" Gertie asked.

Chloe throat went dry and her blood pounded in

her veins as she waited for the answer.

"In the shop."

"Your usual?" The older waitress snapped open her pad and made notes.

"Yeah, but let her bring it to me. I'll train her how to give the customer what he wants."

Chloe bit back a retort. The guy was downright scary, but even so she had to know about the green truck. "Did you have engine trouble? My car needed a new water pump last week."

"Bummer. Naw, I decided to get a little bodywork done. It was looking pretty rough."

Gertie snickered. "Unlike this beauty."

Bubba laughed and temporarily seemed harmless. Chloe's fear of him eased until he gave her a last look. His eyes were cruel even when he smiled. How the hell had Gordy gotten involved with this guy?

"Okay, he liked you. So that went well." Gertie announced when they walked back to the building. Another car pulled in and a woman stuck her head out the window.

"I phoned in."

"Name?"

"Lambert Oil."

And that was the last quiet moment Chloe had. She and Gertie worked out a system. Gertie took their orders; Chloe delivered them. When they flashed their lights, Chloe picked up the trays.

Throughout lunch she watched Bubba's truck. About every twenty minutes, Gertie had Chloe deliver a sandwich or another beer to him. The man could put away food. He ate two beef brisket sandwiches, an order of beef ribs, half a BBQ chicken, potato salad, coleslaw, fries and four piping hot fried apple pies.

Not to mention three red draws and two sweet teas.

Unlike other customers in the lot, he stayed. And he had a green truck. This was Gordy's contact. Around twelve-fifty he flashed his lights and she was relieved to go out for the last time.

The big man hadn't said anything to her out of line, but Chloe's sense was that he held back waiting for an opportunity.

"Did you enjoy lunch?"

He grunted. Chloe weighed her options and decided that was a yes. She smiled.

"Why don't you give me your phone number?" He leered at her from the truck window. "You and I could go for a ride some night."

Chloe was experienced in turning men down nicely. Somehow she suspected politeness wouldn't really work with a man like Bubba. It would be like issuing a challenge.

"No way. My old man would smack me around if he found out I was riding around with some other guy." That declaration just set women back about fifty years, but Bubba wasn't into women's rights.

He validated her opinion when he laid his head back and roared out a laugh. But as quickly as the laugh began, it ended. His attention was focused on a silver car that drove through the lot.

Chloe watched the car exit and heard Bubba's truck roar to life beside her. "Grab this tray. I've got to go."

Chloe did as he asked noticing the fifty-dollar tip. As Bubba rounded the corner headed in the same direction, Chloe took out her pen and jotted the silver car's license plate under Bubba's which she'd written down earlier.

"How come he pulled out of here so fast?" she asked Gertie when she was back inside.

"Who?"

"Bubba."

"He left? Did he tip you?"

"Yeah. Fifty bucks."

Gertie cackled as she snatched orders from the pickup window and loaded them on her tray. "Did he ask you out?"

"Order up. Fifty-two," the black woman hollered through the window.

Fifty-two was hers. She waited for Gertie to move out of the way. "No, but he asked for my phone number."

Gertie sniggered. "Did you give it to him?"

Was she crazy? Of course not. "No."

"Well, you're smarter than you look." Gertie danced out to the parking lot, letting the screen door slam behind her.

Wow, a compliment. Kind of.

# # #

Officer Williams sat in the brown sedan under the shady pecan tree and punched a number into his cell phone.

"Michaels," the voice on the other end answered.

Williams scratched his jaw. "We may have misread this situation. Guess who's working at J Nors and just had a lengthy chat with our boy, Bubba?"

"Who?" Michael's tone assured him of his complete attention.

"The pretty little blonde who's everybody's girlfriend."

"Chloe La Ruse?"

"Yep."

"Well, isn't that an interesting turn of events."

Chapter Twenty Four

Zack hadn't been at Gordy's house half an hour before Glyn showed up, wearing a look of pinched nerves and exhaustion. The dark circles under her eyes testified to her lack of sleep.

"Thanks for coming." He kissed her cheek. Glyn's smile waned as she leaned against her brother. With deep sigh she clung to him. The last time she'd needed his support had been following Arnie's death.

"The police are at the house talking to Mom." She rubbed her neck. "I'm grateful you called. Rehashing the story of Saint Gordon was more than I could take."

He understood. He didn't want to hear their mom's version of reality either. "Headache? Want me to rub your neck?"

"The aspirin will kick in soon."

He hoped so. He hated to see her in pain. But as complicated as yesterday had been, he wasn't sure aspirin would cure all of her problems. "Gordy's got to be out of here by the end of the month. Unless you want some of this stuff I thought we'd just pile it together on the porch and call Goodwill."

Glyn shrugged. "Other than the car, I doubt he owned anything of value."

"Chloe thinks we'll find money and drugs stashed around the house, so look for hiding places."

Glyn snorted. "Every dime went into that car. But I'll go through the pockets of his clothes."

The sparsely furnished décor validated Glyn's statement. The dining room, devoid of furniture, was not the only empty room. The living room housed only a battered couch and coffee table, the kitchen had a few pots and pans, dishes, a coffee pot, a toaster and in lieu of a table, two barstools.

But his bedroom, the only one of three with possessions testified to the fact that Gordy occasionally spent the night.

A flat-panel television and a computer lined one wall. The matching king-size bedroom set was made of cheap fiberboard. Other than the closet packed with clothes nothing personal decorated the shelves or walls. Zack opened a couple of black plastic trash bags.

Glyn surveyed the room. "He's tidier than I would have guessed."

"Yeah," Zack agreed, though he suspected some of Gordy's tidiness came from Chloe's earlier paper harvesting. Why hadn't she taken the computer? He sat down in front of it and booted it up while scanning the software cases on the shelf. All games. No generic products for word processing or accounting spread sheets.

The computer was not password protected, fortunately. He scanned applications and found several racing games along with the usual war game like Call of Duty.

"Nice clothes," Glyn said, interrupting his thoughts. "Do we know anybody who could use them?"

Zack bit his tongue, choosing not to point out the strong objection people might have to a drug-dealer's wardrobe. "I don't."

"Me either." Glyn hoisted a stack of pants from the closet. "Were your feelings hurt by what Velda said?"

"About Arnie not being my father?"

"Yeah."

Was he? He didn't think so.

"Not really. I think I already knew. What difference does it make? Arnie treated me the same as he did you and Gordy." He'd been surprised himself by how little her statement had bothered him. But he hadn't invited his sister here to talk about his problems. "Whose idea was it to put off the wedding? I thought you were gung-ho yesterday."

Glyn folded another pair of pants before she answered. "Planning a wedding is kind of like the proverbial snowball. Once it hits the downhill slope there's no stopping it. I was caught up in the myriad of events. Until Gordy's death I hadn't stopped to consider what I wanted."

"The Houston job?"

She laughed, a self-depreciating sound. He turned from the computer monitor to see her face, but she'd already stepped back into the closet. She returned with another armload of clothes which she threw on the bed and turned her intent brown gaze on him. "A couple of years ago, mom began self-medicating."

Zack's face must have betrayed his surprise, because she immediately added. "Prescription drugs. Her behavior became erratic. So much so, I complained to her doctor which, as you can imagine, infuriated her. She changed doctors, hid her prescriptions and became more psychotic than ever. I had to get out. So I applied for jobs elsewhere."

Each item of clothing was checked, folded and placed into the plastic bag as she spoke. Glyn projected an efficiency that he admired.

He examined each software case before adding it

to the growing pile in another bag. "Is it still going on?"

"It's worse than ever. She's paranoid beyond belief. Hardly an hour goes by that she doesn't fly off the handle at some minor incident. About a month ago, the bank put her on probation. I don't know what she'd do if she got fired. Mother, of course, blamed it all on the stress of my wedding."

He nodded his head as if he wasn't surprised at all. "And this has been going on for two years?"

"No." She expelled a slow breath. "Arnie's death triggered it. But she's been out of control for the past two years."

He swore under his breath. "Arnie died almost fifteen years ago."

"I know. That stiff upper lip she maintains is the result of more pharmaceuticals than Elvis took. She won't listen because she believes prescription medication won't hurt her."

"And the job in Houston?"

"I told Stanley I was leaving. He panicked, begged me to marry him. I was still considering my answer when Mom and Stanley booked the Church. After that everything became a blur."

Zack pursed his lips to keep from making a rude sound that reflected his true opinion. Glyn was an adult. He hated she was being bullied, but even as an easy-going child, she could only be pushed so far.

He crawled under the table to unhook the computer wires. "I thought Stan didn't like Mom."

"He hates her almost as much as he hates being called Stan," she said, emptying the pockets of a pair of black slacks. "Look a twenty. Chloe was right."

He rose from the floor, holding a group of multi-colored cables in his hand. "Her expectations are higher than that."

"No doubt," Glyn murmured. Zack's head snapped up to look at her.

"Oh, calm down. I didn't mean anything."

"So, Stanley hates Mom, yet has no problem using her to get his way?" Zack placed in the bag with the software.

"That's callous, but basically, what happened. I didn't protest, but that was the last time they agreed. Since then I've been the mediator between my mother and my future husband."

Zack snorted. "You're the bride. Everybody has to do what you say."

The desk drawers were empty. Chloe had been very thorough in her search. Glyn blew air through her closed lips making a sputtering sound.

"Zack, I hate pastels and my wedding colors are pink and lavender. That's how effective my decision-making has been. I never wanted a big wedding."

He unhooked the television. "And Stan did?"

"His parent's guest list was three-hundred-seventy-five people. Most are local. Mom's was a close runner-up with around two hundred sixty."

"How large was your list?"

"Twenty-two."

"Ouch."

"Don't misunderstand me Stanley has a lot of qualities I admire. He's even-tempered and takes care of his parents. But he'll never agree to leave Riggers as long as his parents are alive.

So eleven months after I applied for a nursing position in Houston, MD Anderson called with an offer. Gordy was still alive, I was getting married in two days, but I didn't refuse the position. Wednesday night I couldn't sleep. Not because I was excited about the wedding, but I kept thinking the job offer was a lifeline. Is that pathetic or what?"

Zack shook his head. "I'm sorry."

"You're sorry? Why? I thought it was just a bad case of pre-wedding jitters." Glyn said.

"Then Gordy died Thursday morning. After you and Chloe left, Mom and Stanley had a row largely about who got to be my boss. That's when I knew. I was done."

"You don't love him?"

"In some ways, but there are things I don't understand." Glyn stared out the window.

"Such as?" He couldn't decide if he wanted her to mention their sexual arrangement or not. While he might have found it a fascinating conversation with his teammates, some of whom were definitely into kink, talking with his sister about her sex life had an ick factor he didn't think he could overcome.

"Do you know Stanley won't tell me how much money he makes?"

He breathed a quiet sigh of relief that her issues were financial. "Why?"

"He says I don't need to worry about it."

Zack wasn't sure what to say so he made a noncommittal grunt and hoisted the flat screen off the wall. When he'd stalled as long as possible, he asked. "That's a deal breaker for you?"

"The salary thing? No, but the obligatory thing bothers me." Glyn disappeared back in the closet. "Marrying Stanley would be like being a minister's wife. My life would be a constant sense of duty."

He didn't want to know. He swore he didn't want to know, but he had to ask. "Did you know Stanley was dating another woman right up until the time he proposed?"

"He told you about Lydia?"

"Lydia? I met a woman named Fran."

"Fran? He dated Fran?" She stomped into the closet mumbling something that sounded like "lying bastard." Zack wasn't sorry he told her because she needed to know, but he hated causing her more pain.

When she came out with another armload of clothes, she said, "I wonder if he was lying about Chloe when he told me she came on to him."

Zack choked back a laugh. "Chloe understands everything about sex and nothing about men and women. She's the most repressed woman I've ever met. She would never have come on to Stan. Or any other man for that matter."

Her eyes widened. "You're kidding?"

He shook his head.

"And yet she's slept with two of my brothers. How do the Pritchard men get to be so lucky?" She disappeared back into the closet.

His brother had a lot of clothes. Glyn pulled out another armload. He stripped the bed throwing the linens into another black bag. Because he didn't believe Chloe was wrong, he hoisted the mattress and carried it to the living room, followed by the box springs. Gordy wasn't hiding his money under the mattress.

Glyn pulled clothes out of the dresser drawers. "Are you going to break all this furniture down?"

"No, I'll let Goodwill do that. Is the closet empty?"

At her nod, he stepped into the closet and looked

for possible hiding places. He couldn't imagine how Glyn could've considered such a nebbish guy. With anyone other than his sister Zack wouldn't have cared, but he was glad she'd backed away from him in time.

# # #

Chloe left J Nors and headed to the courthouse. Almost two o'clock. Gertie had pressed her to work through dinner, but Chloe had begged off, halfway afraid Gertie would fire her. But so what?

Today she'd learned most of what she needed to know.

Gertie didn't fire her; she gave her hours for the lunch shift every day this week. Chloe made eighty-seven dollars in tips. She hadn't fumbled the job and if it hadn't been for the painful ache in her feet it was a welcome change from being in school. She sniffed her clothes and got a whiff of onions and smoke. Not all change was good.

An hour in the county records office gave her the names of everyone who owned property on Highway 369 within three miles of the accident. None of the information shed any additional light on Gordy's murder.

Chloe pondered what her next step had to be, but the fantasy of a hot bath and a good book captured her attention and obliterated all thought of Gordy's murder. Weary she grabbed the railing and pulled herself up each step.

The apartment was unlocked. Disappointment hit her in waves. Not only was Zack home, he had company.

Detective Michaels stood in front of her white

board studying her drawings of the accident. He turned as she entered.

"Well, well, look who's here," Thompson said dryly. "Nancy Drew."

Zack was under the sink. All she could see was his headless body stretched out on the kitchen floor. Dinner smelled like chicken. She perked up. Never had a man cooked dinner for her. Then he sat up and she saw the black thunderclouds in his eyes.

"What are you doing?"

"Your sink drains slowly. T-dawg tells me you have a new job. Why don't you tell us about it while I put dinner on the table?" His voice held a dangerous edge, part anger and part something else. He rose to his feet and turned his back to her. She heard water running.

The table was set for three. Chloe set her purse on the counter.

She removed three glasses from the cabinet and a tray of ice from the freezer. "What do you want to know?"

Thompson hung over the bar watching them work. "Everything," he said. "For instance, did Gordy have any enemies?"

Zack bent down to open the oven door as Chloe moved to the sink. His quiet behavior made her edgy. If the other man left, they would talk.

"Obviously he did or he wouldn't be dead," Chloe said. "But do I know any of their names? No."

"He'd been in a fight sometime last weekend," Zack reminded her, his voice sounded much calmer, infuriating Chloe.

"A fight?"

Chloe sighed. "According to Gordy, Dwayne Hollister jumped him in a dark alley. I only have water or beer."

"Water's fine."

Chloe pulled the handle of the faucet adjusting the water to cold. The water drained quickly no longer standing in her sink. She stood transfixed. What had she just said? Dwayne Hollister attacked Gordy. The glass of ice slipped from her hand and shattered in the sink. Dwayne Hollister.

"Are you okay?" Both men asked in unison. Zack moved to the sink to check on her, but Chloe ignored both him and the broken glass and ran to open her purse.

"Look at this." She pulled the paper she'd worked on at the courthouse and hurried to the white board. "DJ Hollister owns the land on either side of 369 from one intersection to the next exactly where Gordy was killed." She marked it in red ink on the white board.

Thompson scratched his jaw. "You're sure?"

Chloe raised an eyebrow and pursed her lips. Even he recognized a teacher's censure and backed down. "Why would Gordy be out at that time of night? The B&L closes at twelve-thirty on weeknights. He wouldn't just drive around for four hours and magically end up in front of Hollister's place. Plus we know Gordy wasn't at the B&L on Thursday night."

Zack placed the chicken on the table. "So what do you imagine happened?" She didn't miss his slight emphasis on the word imagine and gulped. Seeing Zack annoyed was more frightening than dealing with Bubba.

She tapped the intersections with the capped end

of the marker. "Gordy had to have been killed earlier, long before four in the morning. Could the road have been barricaded to prevent traffic between these two intersections?"

Thompson studied her accident board. "The coroner agrees with you. He's estimates death at least twelve to fifteen hours before we pulled him out of the wreck. You've come up with a believable explanation of why it didn't get reported. How'd you know about Junior's?"

Chloe revealed the entire Bubba story including his sudden departure.

Zack didn't say a word, just continued getting dinner ready, but he listened to every word. The glances she flitted his direction kept tabs on his moves. Never once did he look her way. But just the same she knew.

"So a car pulls through the lot," Sam clarified. "And Bubba follows it out?"

"Yeah. According to the bartender, Bubba's in and out of there every day."

"Damn. I wish we had that plate number."

Chloe opened the notebook. "XYS 425."

Sam shook his head, but a smile curved his lips as he dialed his phone. "I need a plate run."

"Run those three phone numbers, too." Chloe whispered and pointed toward the flip chart.

Thompson raised an eyebrow, but gave the phone numbers also. "Nancy Drew," he said, while they waited for the results. "You're officially off the case."

Was he kidding? She was doing all the work. And getting results. "But I've gotten so far."

"No. All you've done is work out enough details to put yourself in danger." The detective gestured at the table. Dinner was ready. All three sat down.

"Danger, how?"

Thompson held the phone to his ear, waiting. "When you show up at Gordy's memorial service tomorrow afternoon what's ol' Bubba goin' to think?"

"He's going to the memorial service?"

Zack make a choking noise and Chloe turned to look, but his stern face gave nothing away.

"I guarantee you he'll have spies there." The detective said

She narrowed her eyes and wrinkled her brow. "If you've known all about this Bubba character, why haven't you arrested him?"

"Because we think Bubba Henson's the middle man. He's not manufacturing the meth and he's not selling it. We want to take down the entire operation."

For the first time since he'd revealed Gordy's fight with Hollister, Zack spoke. "Bubba Henson? The linebacker?"

Thompson nodded and picked up a piece of chicken. "The one and only."

"I could wear a wire-"

"No." Both men said in unison. Zack placed chicken on Chloe's plate as though she was a child, followed by potatoes and green beans. If he hadn't been so unhappy with her, she would've stabbed him with her fork.

The detective held up his hand for silence. "Okay, got it." He disconnected the call, his gaze traveling between her and Zack. "The phone numbers belong to the B&L, Arthur's and Dixie Roland's cell phone."

"Not Bubba? And the license plate?"

"Telling you would only give you another reason to keep your storyboard going. Within days you'd have enough information to convict him."

Chloe frowned. "Wouldn't that help you?"

"No, it wouldn't. If he sensed he was being watched, we might lose the head guy. Say these words with me, 'I promise not to do anymore police work.'"

Thompson smiled when Chloe said nothing. "Fine, don't say it. But your detective days are at an end."

The testosterone level in the room had peaked. Both men maintained a look of masculine superiority infuriating her. To divert their attention, she asked Zack. "Did you clean out Gordy's house today?"

"Uh-huh. We found nothing of interest. On Monday, Goodwill is picking up everything." He turned to the detective. "Chloe thinks Gordy has money and drugs stashed somewhere."

"Probably." Thompson agreed, nodding his head thoughtfully. "If not the house, then the Ferrari."

Chloe pictured television drug busts in her mind. "I've seen pictures where the drugs were hidden in the doors and running boards."

"Once my guys are finished checking for prints, I'll have them dismantle the car."

Nope, something was off. "You won't find anything."

"Why?"

"Gordy was lazy. That would involve work and might damage the Ferrari, something he'd never risk."

"Where else?" Thompson asked.

Chloe looked at Zack. "I don't know." She shook her head before stabbing a bite of children. It was delicious. The man could cook. She peeked at him from under her eyelashes. Yes, he had more testosterone than the law allowed, but he wasn't a bully. He was considerate, maybe a little overprotective, but… and she admitted this reluctantly… it was nice to be looked after for a change.

# # #

Chloe's nervous little glances in his direction every few minutes, reminded him of her insecurities. Zack had been furious when he found out that she had charged off on her own. Furious, and a little proud if the truth were known. Chloe didn't rely on brute strength to solve her problems.

She was clever and used her brain to her advantage.

It took him by surprise. Glyn and Bernice were related to Gordy and they weren't doing anything to solve his murder. Bernice looked for someone to blame and Glyn treaded water, trying to save herself. If stranded on a desert island with these three women, it'd be Chloe who'd figure out how to build a boat by lashing banana leaves together. It'd be Chloe who'd make him laugh as her mind raced in a dozen different directions. And God knows it'd be Chloe who'd keep him warm at night.

"I probably need to get going," Thompson said. The plates had been cleared, the three of them still sat at the table.

"I'll walk down with you. I want to look at Chloe's car and see if I can get it running,"

"Do you think," Zack addressed Chloe, "that if I go all the way down the stairs and four steps into the parking lot, you can stay out of trouble?" He teased her, hoping for a smile.

Her eyes lit up and a slow, mischievous grin crossed her face. "Why don't I come with you and save you the panic?"

Zack grunted as the three of them headed to the parking lot. Chloe unlocked the car and pulled the hood latch.

"Expensive tires," The detective noted as she got out from behind the steering wheel. Zack raised the hood.

"Gordy," she said simply and peered over the engine to help Zack look.

"When?" Thompson prodded.

"For my birthday a couple of years ago. Back then he drove the car as much as I did."

"He went from driving a forty-year-old Pinto to a Ferrari?" Surprise evident in his voice.

"It's a classic." Chloe pointed toward the far corner. "The battery's new."

Zack shook his head, then scraped at the corrosion crusting the cable with his screwdriver. "Who replaced it for you?"

"Gordy. The car quit running before Christmas break. He kept promising to fix it, but nothing happened until I brought home this battery."

"Why didn't he replace the cables or at least clean them off?"

"He told me that stuff acted as insulation."

Both men guffawed, but Zack asked, "Why did you think it was the battery?"

"The car ran fine." More non-communicative grunts conveyed their disbelief. She rolled her eyes and amended. "Good enough. Then one day it wouldn't start."

The detective pointed. "I wouldn't have said it was the battery, I would've gone with the missing distributor cap."

Zack chose his words with care. "Is there any reason why Gordy wouldn't have wanted you to drive this car anymore?"

Her eyes blinked rapidly in disbelief as she did a double take. "What? No. Why?"

"Because I saw the missing distributor cap in Gordy's garage this afternoon."

"Shit," Thompson said. We need to search this car." Rolling up his shirt sleeve, he swung into working detective mode. "Open it up."

Twenty minutes later all three stood at the open hatchback staring into the spare tire well.

Replacing the missing spare, tire tool and jack were four stacks of hundred dollar bills bundled together as Chloe had predicted, and a dozen or so zip-lock bags full of a white powdery substance, several containers of baking powder, a scale, and another zip-lock bag of metal utensils.

Chloe reached for a stack of money, but the detective grabbed her arm. "Crime scene."

Zack closed his eyes and willed this all to be a bad dream.

"Well, we now know why he was murdered."

Chloe stared. "We do?"

Thompson pointed toward the equipment. "Gordy was cutting the meth before he sold it. Along the way, he cheated his clients and the bank."

"The bank?"

"The middle man, in this case Bubba, is known as the bank."

Chapter Twenty Five

The tow truck hauled the car onto the rear of the flatbed. The Pinto, no one liked but her, was being seized in a drug bust. How dare Gordy include her in his problems? If he were still alive, she'd kill him.

Thompson and Zack wanted to strangle her. In no uncertain terms both had cautioned her about "getting out of line again." Again? When had she been out of line the first time?

Okay, maybe getting the job at J Nors had been a mistake. Oh, damn, she just remembered. "I'm scheduled to work at ten in the morning. Should I just not show up?"

"Yeah."

"Hold on," Thompson said. "We don't want to arouse any suspicions. What time is the memorial service tomorrow?"

"Two-thirty."

"That gives us time. I think you should go to work. Can you act normal?"

"How would I know? I'm not sure what normal is," Chloe said, sounding even to her own ears like a snotty teenager.

"I'm sure that's what T-dawg's counting on." Zack said dryly. "I don't want her used in this. Too dangerous and she's impulsive."

Sam overrode Zack's objections with an easy wave of his hand. Chloe watched Zack's face change from friendly to non-readable. Both men were used to calling the shots. Who would prevail?

"You and I can keep tabs on her from across the street. She has a skill for observation." The detective looked at Chloe, missing the change in Zack's expression.

What a day. This was the second time she'd gotten kind-of a compliment. Instead of rejoicing, she pursed her lips. Pleasing the cop meant nothing to her. It was Zack whose approval she sought. And he wasn't giving it. When she looked his direction he frowned. What had she done now?

"This will probably hurt your feelings," Thompson gestured for the trio to move out of the way of the tow truck driver as he negotiated the tiny parking lot. "But I don't want you to attend the memorial service tomorrow."

Surprisingly enough, her feelings were completely undamaged. The family had been clear they didn't want her there. Zack had walked a thin tightrope not agreeing with his family, but not disagreeing either.

"Will I ever see my car again?" In the dark lot, Chloe stumbled over the curb. With lightening reflexes, Zack grabbed her arm, preventing her from taking a tumble.

"Count your blessings. I'm not following procedure and arresting you as the owner."

"But I didn't do anything." Chloe protested, wondering how men got to be so arrogant.

"Luckily, I believe that." His words were thrown back over his shoulder as he walked toward his car. "See you tomorrow." He nodded at Zack who didn't respond.

Tail lights disappeared around the corner and still Zack hadn't moved.

"What are we going to do, now?"

One corner of his mouth curled in rueful smile.

"It's time for reinforcements." Zack folded his arms across his chest. "I've sat back long enough."

On some men the gesture might have looked defensive, but instead it reminded Chloe of Superman. He just needed an American flag and a cape flickering in the wind. His confidence was absolute.

Move over local law enforcement. This is the man in charge.

"You didn't need reinforcements two days ago when Gordy died." Chloe said, still trying to figure out his plan.

"Nothing I did would bring Gordy back. The police were doing their job and had a plan of attack. I saw no reason to interfere."

The wind kicked up. Dust swirled around the parking lot.

"But now you do? Why?" she reached up to secure her fly away hair in a bunch.

"Because," he leaned over and kissed her lightly, "now they're using you for bait."

# # #

Fifteen minutes later, Zack opened the door to go out. "Lock the door behind me."

"Where are you going?"

"Out."

"When will you be back?

"Later."

"What are you going to do?"

"Nothing."

Chloe threw the wet sponge at him. "I'm not a child, you know."

Zack caught it and crossed the kitchen to where she stood washing dishes. She refused to look at him, facing the window above the sink. He reached around her, dropped the sponge into the soapy water, and flipped the water faucet on high.

Before Chloe had time to react, he whispered in her ear, "I no longer trust that your apartment isn't bugged. I need to make a call and be assured of privacy. Your cooperation would help."

The anger drained out of her. She nodded in compliance.

"It's awful not being trusted, isn't it?"

She should have told him about Gordy's book and her plan. "I'm sorry." Chloe gripped the sink, before forcing herself to face him, but he was already out the door.

She should've told him. Why hadn't she? Because she assumed that he would react like Gordy who would have spent the evening arguing about something she'd already decided to do. Zack was only a short-term fling. But as a lie she couldn't make it work because she knew that he wasn't Gordy. Zack would've listened.

He re-appeared two hours later, his black, sweat-stained t-shirt clung to his muscular chest. She rose from the couch where she'd been preparing her next class.

"What are you watching?"

She glanced at the TV, surprised to see she'd turned it on. "I don't know. The news, I guess."

Zack grinned. It amused him she hadn't been paying attention to television, but still had it turned on anyway. Some nights the quiet apartment got to her, but that wasn't the important issue here. Her impatience overrode her common sense. "Well, what happened?"

Zack grabbed the hem of his t-shirt and pulled it over his head. She clamped her lips together to keep from ogling him. Six-packs abs actually looked like a six-pack. The muscles in his chest and arms were delineated even when he wasn't flexing. With the crumpled t-shirt, he swabbed under his armpits. Until that very moment, Chloe would have declared such an action disgusting. But Zack brought the gesture to a whole new level of sexy.

He looked up, finished with his minimal cleanup. "Nothing, why?"

Her thoughts must have shown on her face, because he suddenly grinned -- a wicked, knowing look that made her toes curl and beads of perspiration break out across her lip.

She grimaced to show her distain but couldn't quite master it. "You're all sweaty."

"Uh-huh," he agreed, taking a step closer. "I went for a run."

Chloe held her hand up to stop him. "For fun?"

"Yeah, and to keep in shape. I usually run ten miles a day."

"I don't know why you work so hard. You can get that same body on sweatyhunks.com."

"I don't think so. No doubt sweaty hunks offers something for money, but not this body. I'm going to take a shower. Come join me."

"I don't think so," she mimicked.

He stepped closer. His scent didn't repel her like she'd expected. In fact she felt her nipples harden and reached up to scratch her neck in a gesture that was designed strictly to hide any evidence of her arousal.

"It's hard for you, isn't it, to share your territory with someone else?" A predatory growl deepened his voice.

Chloe grasped for reasons to keep him at bay. "If the situation was reversed, you'd be the one having the same problems."

He reached for her. "You betcha. I've already peed in all the corners at my place."

"What a delightful thought." She allowed herself to be persuaded to follow him into the bathroom.

Turning on the shower, he spoke in a low voice. "Tomorrow morning I'm leaving early. Can your cab driver friend get you to Juniors?"

"Sure."

"Listen carefully. I need you to follow my instructions exactly. Right after Bubba arrives, get out to his truck as quickly as you can. Wear something that'll keep him occupied, but for sure, chat him up. Do whatever it takes to not let him look out his rear view mirror on the passenger's side."

Chloe nodded. "What are you going to do?"

"Plant a tracking device."

"Don't you need a search warrant for that?"

"T-dawg would. That's why we're not going to tell him," Zack said. "Then get yourself fired. Walk out. Stay to the left. My men will be waiting for you."

"Your men?"

"A few of my guys are going to visit for a couple of days."

Chloe wanted to kick herself for not doing that SEAL research. "Tell me exactly what the SEALs do," she pressed.

"Unconventional warfare, basically counter-terrorism." The PR answer. It told her nothing. Unconventional warfare? Then it dawned on her what he meant.

"Like Guerrilla fighting?"

He nodded.

"Where's the most exciting place you've ever been?"

Zack looked into her eyes and grinned. "Hell, honey, it doesn't get more exciting than Riggers, Texas. You've got beautiful women, sex, murder, drugs, and mayhem."

Chloe rolled her eyes. "Why am I reminded of that Warren Zevon song about sending lawyers, guns and money, the shit has hit the fan?"

He laughed. "You've got something better than lawyers, guns and money. You've got SEAL Team Nine."

"The entire team is coming?"

"No, most are out of the country. Only three guys, but that'll be plenty for what we need."

# # #

The weather turned. The next morning was hot. Spring was over. Within days air conditioners would be turned on and the town would settle in for another miserable summer. She grumbled on the ride downtown. She hated air conditioning. It was too chemical to be good for people or the environment. What was she doing living in a climate that required it?

Phil stopped on the side street and Chloe wandered up the slight incline to the covered parking and the back entrance. Today she'd worn comfortable shoes not wanting to add to the aches and pains from yesterday. As she stepped into the dark dining area, a rough female voice called out. "We ain't open yet."

Chloe searched for the face in the shadows. Two inches of dark roots separated the brassy blonde hair from her scalp. A series of hot oil treatments would have done wonders. Her leathery skin was tough, hardened by a scar from the corner of her eye to her mouth. Flat-chested and bony, the woman had the build of a scrawny, plucked chicken.

The kitchen was surprisingly quiet.

Chloe held out her hand. "You must be Georgia. Gertie hired me yesterday."

"The hell she did." Georgia sprang to her feet and stomping toward the kitchen. "No one poaches on my territory."

Laughter erupted from the kitchen. Apparently they were listening for the initial meeting of the two waitresses. Chloe was grateful Zack insisted this be her last day. She worried last night that she'd have trouble getting herself fired. Staying employed would be the harder task.

The scent of mouthwatering mesquite-smoked meat hit her. Her stomach rumbled. She stuck her head out the door to see who worked the smokers. The black woman poked at the meat with an over-sized fork, flipping the briskets and readjusting the racks of ribs. She stood on a step stool to reach the upper racks.

With a loud clank the metal lid slammed in place. The woman shuffled toward the kitchen giving her a grin, showing several missing teeth. Chloe smiled back.

"Could I get something to eat?"

"What chew want?"

"Anything."

"Sit." She pointed toward the dining room. "I'll bring it."

Chloe grabbed a bottle of water and sat at one of

the tables. Georgia had left her half-finished beer on the counter.

A beef brisket sandwich and a side of slaw arrived. "Thanks."

"Trouble's coming. Gertie's here." The woman warned and shuffled back into the kitchen.

"You hired some big-boob college girl to replace me?" Georgia screamed. Every word could be distinctly heard through the closed door that separated the kitchen from the dining room. Chloe would have been offended by Georgia's insult, but she'd dressed to attract attention.

She'd chosen a shiny little tank top with tiny straps, designed to show both cleavage and a couple of inches of skin at the waist. Until today, she'd always worn another shirt on top.

"Deal with it," was Gertie's hard reply.

Great. That'll make us friends.

"Well, she can't touch my things," Georgia said.

Like I'd want to.

"Or wait on any of my customers."

You can have everyone but Bubba. He's mine.

"Georgia," Gertie's voice held a warning note.

"What!"

"Learn to share. Chloe's working here and so are you."

"Chloe? That's the bitch's name?"

Nope. Friendship was completely out of the question.

She finished her meal, tied her apron and cleaned the dining room, purposely dumping Georgia's beer down the sink. How was she going to wait on Bubba if Georgia claimed dibs?

The bartender showed up, took one look at the situation and mumbled under his breath. Georgia stormed around, acting like she was working, but accomplishing nothing. Gertie ignored everyone and sat at the corner table chain smoking and going through yesterday's receipts.

At eleven sharp, the blue truck pulled into the lot. Chloe worked hard to beat out Georgia.

"Red draw," she said quietly to the bartender.

"No way. He's my customer," Georgia announced loudly. Chloe glanced at the silent Gertie, who pretended nothing was amiss. Was she waiting for them to slug it out? Or did the older woman think she wasn't tough enough to hold her own?

"Fine." She said, "But don't be surprised if he asks for me."

Georgia sloshed a third of the beer snatching it out of Chloe's reach before heading out the door. She'd never fought for a man before and certainly not for one she hated, but Georgia came to this battle unarmed.

As soon as Georgia was halfway across the parking lot, Chloe stepped out of the dining room and walked from under the covered area. Standing in the sunlight, she swayed her hips and waved.

The window lowered and Bubba stuck his head out. "C'mon over here," he yelled. Georgia turned her head. A snarl curled her lips, but she was careful not to say anything to the customer. Both watched Chloe saunter across the lot. Only one happy to see her.

"Hey, Bubba," She said as she got closer.

"Hey, darlin'."

Certain he'd forgotten her name, she caught a movement out of the corner of her eye at the back of the truck, but it was so quick, she wasn't sure she imagined it.

"Nice day, huh?"

Georgia had held her temper for what Chloe assumed was a record amount of time. "You don't need to be out here. There are other customers for you to wait on."

She looked at the empty lot. "I just came out to say hello," Chloe said. "And thank him for the really nice tip he left me yesterday."

Bubba shifted his eyes from one woman to the other. He stuck his finger under the collar of his shirt and ran it around the neck. "It was nuthin'. Your first day and all."

She was pretty sure the fat man was sweating and she enjoyed it. Georgia's red face glowed, her jaw pulsed and her hand curled in a fist.

Go ahead, take a swing.

Lowering her eyelids, she gave Bubba a smile she hoped looked promising.

Whether it did to Bubba or not was uncertain, but Georgia unable to hold back snarled like a rabid wild dog. "You, bitch, you're flirting with my customer."

"Really? Bubba asked me out yesterday."

Bubba's eyes flashed open and he attempted to open the door, at the same instant Georgia's fist took flight. In his hurry the door slammed against Georgia and knocked her off balance. She stumbled and would have fallen if Bubba hadn't caught her arm and held her upright.

"You tried to hit me." She said, trying to summon every piece of indignation she could manage, which was hard since she wanted to throw back her head and laugh.

Taking the mug of beer from the tray, she dumped the red liquid over the top of Georgia, who wailed and would have attacked her if Bubba hadn't grabbed her. Jeez, he was huge. How could Gordy have gotten involved with him?

Chloe could see confusion written all over Bubba's face. Like most men, Bubba knew how to handle males, women who were out of control remained a mystery to him. Particularly since he was being forced to take sides.

"Go on," Bubba said. "You've caused enough trouble." His mean little eyes narrowed. Chloe agreed there was nothing else to say.

Why did men always assume she was the troublemaker? Georgia started it. Inside she untied her apron, dumped it on the counter.

Gertie and the bartender stared at her.

"I'm out of here," were Chloe's parting words. No one made any attempt to stop her.

Chapter Twenty Six

Chloe walked to the corner and stopped. Where were Zack's mysterious men? The right leg of her jeans squished and smelled like beer. Fortunately she'd missed her shirt. Tomato juice stained and she'd hate to throw out a perfectly good shirt.

A dark blue four-door sedan pulled up to the corner. Two men starred at her. Well, what'd she expect dressed like this?

"Chloe?" the man on the passenger's side asked. Did she know them? Why were there only two? Zack had said three. She hesitated.

The passenger opened his car door and the tall man stepped out. Chloe balanced on the balls of her feet prepared to run, if necessary. She looked him over. He obviously shopped at the same store Zack did. His wardrobe selection consisted of dark jeans and a black t-shirt. Zack's basic uniform.

"Operations Officer James Sampson, US Navy. Sorry we're late. You were quicker than we expected." He opened the rear door, saying. "My friends call me Sam or The Cube or S-cubed."

She stared at his arms. His muscles look like twisted ropes. His lean face had a somber look except for two intense blue eyes that burned like gas flames. She guessed this man didn't miss much. "With a name like that math majors must flock to you."

He didn't smile, but his eyes crinkled. "Surprisingly, I don't attract many women who give a damn about math."

"Pity." Chloe was delighted she'd amused him. "Did I give you enough time?"

He shot a look in the driver's direction. "If one

of us hadn't been laughing his ass off, we would've been faster."

"Quite the floor show," the driver extended his hand over the seat back. "Chief Petty Officer Michael Rowe, ma'am."

She scooted across the seat to shake it.

"Call me Chloe. So if Sam Sampson is S-cubed, don't tell me they call you Mike?" she asked as Sam reseated himself.

"Actually, my friends call me Skid." Mike grinned. "As in Skid Rowe."

It was hard to tell his height, but he was shorter, more compact than his teammates. His face was open, not hard in the way of the others. His close cut hair was carrot red and his face sported a bazillion freckles. Mike was a friendly guy if one wanted conversation. Zack was a man a girl took home to bed even if Sam was the better looking of the two, with thick, wavy golden brown hair and a killer smile in a tanned face. The car rolled across the street and parked in an empty spot. Why weren't they moving?

"Why are we sitting here?"

"Waiting for Demon."

Chloe's eyebrows shot up. "Demon?"

Mike and Sam exchanged a look then turned their heads at exactly the same time to study her.

"Zack," Skid clarified.

"He's called Demon?"

Both men wore startled expression as though they'd given her the secret handshake by mistake. "Short for speed demon from his racing days in NASCAR," The Cube said.

"Of course." Chloe nodded and hid a smile when

the tension left the two men's faces.

"While we're waiting why don't you tell me all about BUD/S and Hell week?" She'd spent enough time in front of a computer before she'd left home that morning so that she could dribble SEAL terminology into the conversation.

"BUD/S stands for Basic Underwater Demolition/Seals. Intense basic conditioning." Skid explained. "Hell week comes early in training because only about twenty-five percent remain at the end and the Navy doesn't want to invest in those who aren't going to make it. Generally the first leg of training is jokingly considered two weeks and a long day. The long day is Hell Week and it is not misnamed. By the end of the week over seventy percent of the class have rung out."

"Rung out?"

"To quit you ring a bell three times and place your helmet in a long line. It reminds all of us who stay of the determination and endurance that being a SEAL requires."

Sam nodded, adding, "Hell week is five and a half days of strenuous continuous training on only four hours of sleep. You're wet. You're colder than you've ever been in your life. You're covered with sand while going up against insurmountable odds. It's nothing you forget. You develop this walk known as the Hell week shuffle to keep your salt-stained clothing away from your poor old chafed skin." Both men laughed in memory.

"If it's underwater stuff, why did Zack tell me the SEALs were unconventional warfare, basically counter-terrorism?"

Skid grinned. "Because it's accurate. SEALs is an acronym for sea, air and land. We operate wherever we're needed."

"You both made it so for you it must have been a good experience."

Sam snorted and Mike sighed, but it was Sam who spoke. "I would say we're both proud we made it, but a good experience? The Navy tests your limits. We made it because we had each other as swim buddies. But the Navy brass had told both of us in no uncertain terms we weren't SEAL material and wouldn't make it."

Chloe was fascinated. "So how did you prove them wrong?"

"Like I said, under those circumstances, you learn a lot about who you are," Sam said. "In high school I was a quarterback and was passed along despite the fact my reading skills were non-existent because I was a star player. Skid aced every test but he struggled with most of the training exercises. He taught me to read. I helped him build up his strength."

Mike pivoted his head to watch her expression. "Hell week is hard for everybody. Sam was more prepared for the physical strain, but he'd gotten to where he was by operating as a lone cowboy. I passed because I had endurance and teamwork."

"Were your families proud?"

There was another gap in the conversation while each considered his answer.

"My brother was a Marine gunnery sergeant. He lost a leg in Iraq around the time I made it through. Their attention was more on him, rightly so, than me."

"I haven't seen my parents in a while. My dad's dead and I have no idea what my mother thinks."

Both Sam's tone and words were conversation killers, but Skid continued unfazed, "Sam's adopted brothers are both SEALS. You'll meet Austin. Travis heads another team that is on a training mission."

"OCONUS."

Both men grinned. "Exactly."

The car door opened and Zack slid inside. "Scoot over," he nudged Chloe with his knee and then threw an arm around her shoulders, keeping her from going too far. "You were great. Thompson's pissed but he'll get over it."

Chloe smiled pleased she'd done what he'd requested. "Now what?" she asked eager to continue.

"Phase two." He nodded toward Skid who'd pulled away from the curb. "We wait and see who makes the next move."

Skid drove straight to her apartment without asking for directions. Even though there were spaces available in the lot he circled around the block and parked in back. No one opened the car doors. The Cube and Skid bent forward, their gazes focused on her apartment windows.

"We're good to go," The Cube said, sitting back.

"Do we need to dart behind trees and wave each other on?" Chloe asked. Zack's teammates snickered.

"No. We're going to walk inside like normal people."

Chloe raised an eyebrow. "Are you going to issue me a weapon?"

"After that demo with the beer, you'd be dangerous with a weapon." His lips quirked as though he repressed a smile. Obviously, he thought she was funny.

"I need a nickname."

"What'd you think Nancy Drew was?" he asked.

Chloe grimaced. "Not all nicknames are complementary. Just ask Skid here."

# # #

Zack was pleased to see the new door installed when the A-man opened it.

Chloe, not so much. "Why do I have a new door?" She whirled to face him.

He gently pushed her inside and closed it behind her. "You needed it."

"No, I didn't. The other one closed. Locked. It kept everyone out. But you."

"Precisely."

Chloe pushed past the men and stormed down the hallway. "Stop trying to run my life." The slamming bedroom door shook the glassware in the cabinets.

"Demon, don't you dare leave me here alone again. Every book she owns is about sex. With pictures," Austin, the A-man, pleaded.

Zack laughed. "It's her major." The other men's faces lit up.

"Oh, man, you've fallen in the clover. She's beautiful. She's funny. And she likes sex." His team grinned.

"Show us the books," The Cube said

"She's unbelievably smart. So watch what you say to her." He looked over the A-man's shoulder at the monitor. "Has Bubba gone anywhere?"

"No."

"It's one o'clock. He should be on the move soon. I have to get dressed for my brother's memorial service. Cube, you're my backup.

His men looked uncomfortable. They wanted to say something in condolence, but Zack hurried out of the room to avoid the comments. The afternoon would be difficult enough as it was.

As he stepped out of the shower, Chloe's voice reached him from the living room. Apparently her anger had passed. Walking down the hall to the second bedroom to dress, he heard her ask, "Do you wear this brown and green goo on your faces all the time? Because let me tell you now, I'm not wearing it."

He stuck his head in the living room to see Chloe seated at one of the computer screens.

Obviously she'd pulled up one of the SEALs websites. His men rushed to assure her that there'd be very little jungle warfare in Riggers.

Instead of closing the door, he left it open to hear the conversation. Chloe was funny. He hadn't realized how much he enjoyed listening to her observations. Her voice had a pleasant lyrical quality that lacked the flat Texas twang omnipresent in this area.

"Do you need to get dressed?" Cube asked.

"For what?" she asked.

"The memorial service. Aren't you going with Zack?"

"The police think I've behaved too badly and his family hates me."

Zack strained to hear her words.

"His family hates you? Why?" A-man asked.

"His mother found it easier to blame me than to question her son and his sister got angry because her boyfriend asked me out."

Zack stopped buttoning his jacket and raised his voice so she could hear him. "Stanley asked you out?"

"Uh-huh,"

Zack leaned against the living room door jamb. "He told Glyn you approached him. When did this happen?"

Chloe looked up from her computer screen. "Last winter. Like two weeks before they got engaged."

"Stan didn't mention the other women to Glyn? Why did you tell her?"

"What am I, an idiot? Gordy was here when Stanley called. I never would have told Glyn, but Gordy made sure she knew. You know, in many ways, Gordy wasn't happy unless he was stirring up trouble."

Zack thought about that statement. Probably true. "Would you have gone if it hadn't been for Gordy?"

"Ewww, no. Stanley's such a sycophant. I can't stand him."

"I hate sycophants, too," the Cube declared. "What's a sycophant?"

The A-man stared at one of the three computer monitors that sat on the dining room table. "Ass-kisser."

Cube held up three fingers like the Boy Scout oath. "I'm not, I swear."

"I wasn't accusing you, I was defining the word. A sycophant is an ass-kisser."

Zack stood in the doorway, rhythmically slapping his doubled up belt in his hand. After a few moments of silence, he spoke. "Do a little computer digging. Let's see what comes up on Bubba Henson and Dixie Roland, the waitress at the B&L."

"Dwayne Hollister, too," Chloe added. Zack nodded in agreement.

"Bubba's on the move. He left the parking lot at

Southwest Halston and Klimer. Headed north. He's turning west on Colton Road. Guess who's right on his tail?"

Chloe stood over A-man's shoulder and looked. "You put a tracking device on Detective Michael's car?"

Zack shrugged. "I had an extra one."

Her eyebrow rose. "Well, at least I know when they arrest me, I won't be going to jail alone."

Chapter Twenty Seven

Zack's family remained ensconced behind the closed-door room while the mourners gathered in the sanctuary. Thirty-to-forty relatives crammed into the tight space designed with enough seating for ten. An obituary in the newspaper indicated Gordy died as a result of an automobile accident.

He stood at the chapel door, greeting everyone who came inside. While he had to endure many words of condolence, he also got to speak to everyone who was attending. Most were kids about Gordy's age, old high school friends. Some were neighbors and teachers. Dixie didn't show, neither did Bubba. A few asked about Chloe.

Above him, Cube surveyed the surrounding parking lot and adjacent streets from a hidden location on the roof.

Organ music filled the small chapel and his family filed out of the waiting room and into the empty pews reserved in front. A soprano sang "Ave Maria." Zack shook his head. Not a song Gordy would have chosen. He would have preferred something like Queen's, "Another One Bites the Dust." In fact, "Ave Maria" was the kind of song he would have ridiculed. As the last family member passed, Zack turned to take his place at the end of the line. A flash of bright light caught his eye. Probably nothing, but he didn't believe in coincidence.

He faded into the shadows to search the street through the open doors. There it was again.

He waited, clicking his microphone. "Cube?"

"I see it," came the reply. "White, Ford F-350,

King Cab with gooseneck hitch."

"Got it." Zack watched and waited. Several minutes passed. The soprano sang Amazing Grace.

The truck door opened. The driver, in cowboy garb consisting of boots, jeans, a plaid shirt and a straw hat, walked toward the church. He lacked the bowed gait of a working cowboy or ranch hand and the slouch in his posture gave the impression of a man in his late forties or early fifties.

The cowboy tugged his weather beaten hat further down on his brow, obscuring his face.

"Good afternoon," Zack extended his hand like a greeter and stepping out of the shadows as soon as the man entered the building. The cowboy raised his head. Hostility flickered briefly in his eyes. The emotion didn't catch him off guard but the cowboy wasn't much older than Gordy.

Automatically, the stranger shook hands. Rough large hands, Zack noted. "I hope I'm not too late," the man said.

"Not at all, Mr...."

"Hollister."

Bingo. Thompson Michaels had been right on the money. Here was Bubba's mole. Plus Zack was willing to bet the flash he seen had been off binoculars. Zack forced a smile and gestured for the other man to proceed through the open doors to the chapel. Dwayne outweighed his brother by a good fifty pounds. The fight between them had hardly been fair. Before this was over, if Hollister was involved in any way with Gordy's death, Zack vowed to orchestrate a fight Dwayne would never forget.

"How'd you know Gordon?"

"Mutual friends," Dwayne mumbled.

"Good of you to come." He left him in the rear of

the chapel and headed down the aisle to his family as the minister rose to speak.

He slid in the front pew beside Glyn. Stanley sat on her far side holding his sister's hand.

The minister's scripted eulogy had his mother's fingerprints all over it. The forty-five minute glowing tribute was not to the real Gordy, but to the fantasy child of Bernice's imagination. The perfect son. Zack lowered his eyes unable to make contact with anyone he knew. The least Gordy deserved was to be remembered for who he really was. As the minister finished his final remarks, he invited the guests to come to the front of the chapel and offer private words to the family.

Mourners surrounded Zack. The press of bodies against him was suffocating. His hand was shaken and his shoulder patted more times than he could count. Women hugged him, wrapping him in clouds of sickly sweet perfume. All he wanted was to leave. Finally the crowds thinned and the family trickled out the exit.

Bernice and Velda walked ahead of him. "That went very well," his mother said.

His restraint cost him. He'd intended to watch the departing crowd for suspicious behavior. Instead he studied the floor and prayed he could make it to his car without lashing out at his mother's selfish stupidity.

Bernice turned before she reached the door. "There'll be people coming to the house. Glynnis and I are going to need your help."

His mother was in her element. The queen entertained. Zack managed to not snap at her, reminding himself, she was mourning, too.

Glyn saved him. "I have to go to work, Mother."

"What? You took off this entire week for the wedding."

"Since I agreed to the job in Houston, I have a bunch of stuff to do in order to be ready to leave."

Stanley took Glyn's arm possessively. "Perhaps, we should stop by your mother's house for a little while."

Bernice favored Stanley with a slight curl of her lips.

Glyn pulled back, bumping into Zack. "No. I have other commitments."

"I do, too," Zack seconded. Glyn straightened her posture at his words. They stood together united.

"Of course, you're coming," Bernice snapped. She bit down on her folded tongue, a sure sign of her anger.

His sister trembled. It was a gesture they'd seen since their childhood. It surprised him that it still had power over Glen.

"No, we're not." Zack took Glyn's other arm and guided her through the crowd and out the door.

"That will set her off," Glyn murmured. "Stanley will be angry, too."

"Tough." Zack gave her a quick kiss on the cheek when they reached her car. "I'll talk to you tomorrow." Eager to get away, he hurried to his rental car. Gordy needed a fitting tribute. There was only one place he would have respected.

Zack drove to Arthur's track.

It'd been fourteen years since Zack raced the track. He climbed out of the car and gave the place a quick once over. A lot of things had changed since his last run on the track.

Arthur didn't say hello. His glance pigeonholed Zack with a single look. "You've bulked up. How much do you weigh now?"

"Two twenty-five." Just like that Zack was fifteen again, with Arthur the only adult in charge. He'd spent three years here and never once had Arthur made him feel like anything other than an immature punk. And he re-enforced it by calling him kid.

"We have a two forty weight limit, you know."

Zack grinned. "I'm not looking for a career here. I just wanted to run the track a couple of times in one of your Formula One cars. I'll need a helmet, too."

"And shoes." Arthur leaned over the counter and eyed his footwear. "You can't feel the controls in those clodhoppers."

"Fine. But I'll buy those."

"Fine."

Both men grinned, each glad to see the other.

"Which track did Gordy like to run?"

"Number eight." Arthur gestured with his hand toward the track's location. "You'll never beat his time. Your brother was fast."

"Yeah." Zack nodded. "Gordy probably would have made a good NASCAR driver."

Arthur snorted. "Maybe, if that had been his goal."

He raised his head, his eyes narrowing. "He didn't want to drive for NASCAR?" Arthur was as direct and opinionated as always, but Zack had rarely found him to be wrong.

Arthur shrugged and pointed at him. "Gordy talked about it. But he didn't want it. His real goal was to beat you at just one thing."

"What?"

"Yep. Once Gordy established the best time on track eight, he never ran another track. He refused to race when we set up competitions. NASCAR wasn't his dream, any more than professional Indy car driving was mine."

Zack leaned his elbows on the counter. "But you built this track."

"In the middle of nowhere. If I'd wanted to make this go, I'd have built it in the Dallas-Ft. Worth area. I wasted my youth being angry because fate conspired against me to keep me from my destiny." Arthur chuckled in memory. "Then one day, this skinny fifteen-year-old kid shows up. He forced me to challenge him, to set up races, to make the tracks harder, to get faster cars. He was never satisfied. Always wanted a bigger challenge. That's when I knew. I'd never become a professional because I didn't want it enough. That kid wanted it. And he wasn't going to be satisfied until he was the best."

Zack understood. "That's how I felt about becoming a SEAL."

"Kid, that's how you felt about becoming a NASCAR driver at one point, too. You made me see that anything worth having is never easy. You got to want it with every fiber of your being. I never saw anyone go after something with such determination."

"Yeah, but I never made it as a driver."

"You would have."

Zack shrugged. "Maybe."

"Sorry you quit?"

"No. I'm sorry the Navy's promoting me to a desk job."

"Were you the Honor Man in your class?" Arthur

peered at Zack. The most distinguished graduate, the Honor Man. Funny that Arthur knew. It was Zack's greatest award along with getting his Budweiser, the SEAL pen.

"Yeah, I was. For a wily old coot you know a lot about SEALs."

"My best friend was KIA. Vietnam. One of the green men. A SEAL. I've done research. What are you going to do when you get out?"

"How do you know I'm thinking about getting out?"

"Cause you'd go postal if you had to sit behind a desk all day. Some men would take to it like ducks to water, but you've got a find a position where you challenge yourself to be the best. Every single day."

Zack looked away. "You're right. I've thought about it." In fact, he'd thought about very little else in the past year and a half. "There's a difference between being an adrenaline junkie and finding something challenging. Friends of mine have gone on to teach ski diving or become smoke jumpers. I like being behind a wheel."

"There's a new race team forming in Indianapolis. The owner's a friend of mine. He's looking for a driver."

"How do you know I still have the chops?"

Arthur guffawed. "Son, I thought we just got through discussing that."

An Indy driver. Challenging. Edgy. Strenuous. A smile he couldn't hide curled his lips. "I'll think about it."

Arthur scowled. "If you're going to run the track you'd better hurry, I close in fifteen minutes."

Gordy's record was on number eight. He had no reason to run that track.

"Thanks, think I'll skip it, but I'll send you a plague honoring Gordy's time. You'll hang it?"

"You betcha, kid. Thanks for dropping by."

"I'll see you before I leave."

Chapter Twenty Eight

Zack pushed open the door to Chloe's apartment jam-packed with old fashioned furniture, sex books and sticky notes on every surface. Interestingly, she didn't need post-its to remind of anything regarding school. All her notes were motivational. Who needed that kind of inspiration? A woman who feared the future? But she had her life all mapped out. He shook his head.

Chloe sat alone at the dining room table, now housing A-man's computer, wearing one of the SEALs headsets. She gazed unseeing at the wall.

"Where's everyone?"

Chloe turned her head and lifted her gaze to meet his. Her lips curled but her warm eyes didn't reflect joy. Such a beauty. Yet she had no clue. Gordy had been a fool -- able to be here with her and too stupid not to bind her to him. Or maybe she was never meant to be Gordy's girl.

When he left for California, Thompson would make a move. He'd practically said as much in the car this morning. Chloe had spent her life with her head buried in her books, but no longer. Now she was on every man's radar. If he hadn't staked a clear claim, there would've been infighting among his team.

"They left you here alone?"

"No. I'm on the baby monitor," she groused, pointed to the headset. "They're at the park two blocks away." She pulled the headset off her ears and spoke into the microphone. "Zack's here. I'm signing off now." Without waiting for an answer she clicked the microphone off and tossed the headset to the desk.

He picked up the activity report on the afternoon's events. "Where's everyone now?"

Chloe pointed to the screen. "Bubba and Dwayne are each at home. Sam's at the police station."

Zack turned his attention to the computer screen. "What are you doing?"

"Thinking."

Zack pulled up a dining room chair and sat beside her. "About?"

The tip of her tongue touched the side of her mouth as her eyes studied the keyboard. "If I wanted to search for someone, but didn't want your guys to know it, how would I do it?"

Zack placed his fingers over the keys and waited. "The first thing we'd do is type in a name and see what comes up."

"Paula Marie La Ruse."

Zack said nothing as he entered the name. No matches in Google. Zack typed in a code and a different scene came up. "Address?"

She watched him work. "Don't know."

"Age?"

"Forty-two."

Again nothing. Zack touched the keyboard again with a different code.

"What else do you know?"

"She was born here."

Zack typed for several minutes. A birth certificate came on the screen. Zack scanned it.

Paula Marie La Ruse was not a distant relative. "Is this your mother?"

"Yes." Chloe's eyes were bright and she blinked a couple of times.

Zack read the screen. "When was the last time you heard from her?"

"Twenty-four years ago."

She hadn't heard from her mother in twenty-four years? Zack said nothing, but typed another series of letters and numbers. He worked to keep his face impassive. When that code didn't help, he entered another. And then another. Damn, he didn't want to ask. "Are you sure she's still alive?"

Chloe slumped in the chair. "There's a Bambi La Ruse who's an exotic dancer in Vegas. I thought that might be her."

Zack typed some more. "According to this Bambi La Ruse's real name is Carmen Soloman, age thirty-four, originally from Santa Barbara, California."

"What data base are you in?"

"IRS."

"Really?" Chloe sat quietly. "You can't find anything on my mother?"

Zack wanted to hold her. But with her arms folded across her chest, she didn't want sympathy. And after this afternoon, he could understand that. "I'm sorry."

"Wouldn't there be a death certificate?"

"Not necessarily." He hated giving her bad news.

She sat quietly for a few minutes and then she rose. "Well, I guess I don't have any family. I supposed that means I need to quit fooling around and finish my thesis." She walked to the kitchen and got a glass out of the cabinet.

"Why'd you think your mother was a stripper?"

She filled her glass with water and took a long drink. "Exotic dancer," she corrected automatically. "Gramps and Gram would never talk about her. I figured she must have embarrassed them in some way. And when I came across the name Bambi La Ruse, I wanted it to be her."

Zack heard a key in the door. His team had returned. Zack quickly shut down the screen as his three man team came inside. All looked exhilarated from their work out. They grinned at Chloe as they lounged on the couch and the chair. She frowned, still peeved about the baby-monitoring headset.

Zack ignored the interplay. "What'd you dig up on the people I asked about?"

"The waitress, Dixie Roland's a single mother with a kid and her bank account's overdrawn. Bubba's real name is Leroy Albert Henson. He owns nothing. No car, no truck, no house registered in his name, declares an income of less than fifteen thousand a year - self-employed sales. Dwayne Hollister, though, is another situation. He had some severe financial problems about six years ago to the point of foreclosure on his ranch. Today, he is not only solvent, but owns the property free and clear despite only declaring an income of about twenty-five thousand from ranching. That truck costs more than a year's income."

Zack puffed out his cheeks and blew air between his lips. "We're going to do a sneak and peek tonight. Get ready."

"What'd you expect to find?" The Cube asked.

"Don't know."

# # #

"Anything?" Chloe mumbled several hours later as Zack crawled into bed.

He wrapped an arm around her waist and she snuggled closer. "Just the green truck with yellow paint on the right front fender. It's in a barn at

Hollister's. Thought you'd be asleep."

"If Bubba doesn't own it, who does?"

"Charlene Henson Roberts, his sister."

"What next?"

"We wait. Sleep, now."

Chloe turned toward him. "You'll be gone in a few days. If I sleep, I might miss something."

She placed a hand on his cheek.

"Like?"

"Like making love to you."

Beneath her fingers, his cheek curl into a smile. He pulled her closer. "Well, that would be tragic."

# # #

Chloe stumbled out of bed the next morning to an empty apartment. The two rental cars were parked behind her apartment. Wherever the men went, it was on foot.

Jeez, where did they get the energy? If Chloe operated on as little sleep as they did, she'd be known as Miss Snappy Panties.

The refrigerator was empty, but the pantry was worse. Feeding four big men was a challenge. A note on the counter caught her attention.

Gone for a run. Z.

She added to the note. *Pick me up at Safeway at ten. C*

Chloe prowled the grocery store aisles looking for bargains. Last night's dinner had been an eye-opener. They'd ordered six large pizzas and eaten every morsel after adding enough red chili flakes to set her intestines on fire. She'd managed to snag two pieces before the pepper flakes were added and had been full after a piece and a half. If this was competitive eating she wasn't even a contender. And not a single one of those men sported one ounce of fat.

A special on chicken had her putting four whole birds into the cart along with five pounds of hamburger and a pork loin. She headed toward the dairy aisle when she heard her name.

Stanley clutched a small white bag from the pharmacy as he trotted across the open space.

She waited.

"Hey, I haven't seen you in ages." he leaned in to kiss her. She turned her face, so he didn't miss her cheek and accidentally hit her lips as he had a few weeks ago.

An awkward silence fell between them. "Too many hard feelings with the family."

Stanley glanced at her shopping cart and then took another look. "Why are you buying all this food? Are you feeding an army?"

She hesitated. With no ready lie available, did it matter if Stanley knew? Zack had probably already told Glyn.

"Some of Zack's friends are in town."

"Friends?"

"You know, guys on his SEAL team." Chloe ignored Stanley and searched the store in case Zack was early.

"Why?" Stanley asked, bringing her attention back to him.

A creepy feeling crawled up her neck. She turned again to be sure she wasn't being watched. "They're helping him figure out who killed Gordy."

"Isn't that what the police are doing?"

"The police know who killed him, but they're

laying a trap for the entire drug ring."

Stanley knitted his brow into one long hairy caterpillar crawling across his eyes. His receding hairline crept further back. He looked fierce not like Stanley at all.

She back-peddled. "Is it called a drug ring? I know they use the word cartel for South American drug lords." She shrugged when Stanley didn't respond. "Anyway. Right now they're waiting to catch the meth manufacturer. Apparently, they don't think Bubba's bright enough for that."

Stanley blinked several times. "I had no idea, Gordy's drug dealing was so… pervasive."

"Are you feeling okay? You're as white as a ghost."

Stanley stared vacantly at her face. Was he seeing her at all? "Stanley?"

He didn't answer.

"Stanley?"

He mumbled something, but she wasn't sure what. She started to ask him, but he walked away.

What's wrong with him?

By the time Chloe had reached the checkout counter, her cart was filled to overflowing. She hoped she had enough money in her account to cover the check she was about to write.

Zack would reimburse her if she asked, but she wanted to do something nice for him before he left.

Moving lethargically she placed each item on the cashier's belt. Her heart thudded. Thinking about Zack's leaving was a mistake. Last night they'd made love. Long, slow and so sweet. Afterward he'd fallen asleep, Chloe had crept into the bathroom and cried into a towel. No words expressed how utterly stupid and depressed she felt. She'd fallen in love with a man who could never be hers.

"One hundred and ninety-five dollars," the cashier said. She bent to write a check.

He'd go back to California. In two months, she'd leave for Indiana. She'd fantasized about making a mark in the world, but Zack had done it. He was keeping the world safe. No wonder Gordy had been both proud and jealous.

When Gram died, Chloe had been alone. Now with Zack leaving not only would she be alone, but heartbroken and impoverished. She didn't spend that kind of money on food for a month. She pushed the basket toward the exit.

Zack appeared beside her. She smiled, trying desperately to not let him see her unhappiness. "Here you are. Wow, you bought a lot of food."

"I figured it was easier to cook for this many than to order pizza and fast food."

"Probably, but we can survive on anything. The stories I could tell."

"If it's about BUD/S or those awful nutritional MREs, I've already heard plenty."

"I'll bet." He loaded the groceries into the trunk and drove the three-block distance to her apartment.

Between the two of them they managed to lug all the bags up the stairs.

"Bubba's on the move," the A-man announced as soon as they entered the apartment. "And unless I miss my guess he's breaking the speed limit to get there. Whoa. And it looks like Dwayne's leaving now, too."

Zack stacked the last of the bags on the counter. "Let's go."

Skid and the Cube were already gathering equipment. A-man stayed at the monitoring controls. Chloe sighed. It looked like she'd be putting the groceries away.

"You coming?"

Chloe checked behind her at the empty kitchen just to make sure he wasn't asking someone else. Her heart leaped. They were including her in the action. A wide grin broke across her face, she shoved the groceries, plastic bags and all into the refrigerator and grabbed her purse. "I'm ready."

"Hold on, Nancy Drew, we've still got a few things to grab. Put on that headset."

Somehow being a part of the team didn't make the nickname Nancy Drew so childish. And the baby monitor now was an important piece of the equipment.

# # #

Zack hid his smile. Chloe had been so down. Inviting her along had been worthwhile just to see her face light up. He doubted that this would turn into anything big. Including her was easy. They took the blue car. Skid drove, listening to the A-man's directions through the headset.

The neighborhood became more industrial. And more sparse.

Zack tossed her a black knit cap. "Cover your hair."

"The next right, you ought to see Bubba's truck." A-man's deep voice spoke into her ear.

"Let's make a lap," Zack said. They drove past. Several vehicles including Bubba's truck, sat next to an orange SUV in front of an isolated metal warehouse.

"Isn't that funny?" Chloe murmured

"What?" They spoke quietly although everyone could hear them over the mics.

"That orange SUV looks just like Stanley's. Did I tell you I saw him this morning at the store? He acted so weird."

"How?"

"He saw all the food in the cart and wanted to know who it was for. So I told him."

"What'd you tell him?"

"Pretty much everything. Then he looked sick and walked away."

"Get Glyn on your cell phone. I want to make sure she's all right." To Skid, he pointed, saying, "Turn in here. We need a strategy."

"Glyn?" Chloe said. "Zack had me call. He wanted to get together with you. Are you at home?"

Chloe listened. "Work? Yeah, that'd be awkward. Hang on, I'll put him on."

"She sounds fine," Chloe whispered and handed him the phone.

"Everything okay?" Zack asked. "Have you heard from Stanley today? … No? Don't call him. I just wondered if he was still angry… I'll bet Mom is. Call me when you're done working…Great to talk to you, too. Love you."

Everyone got out of the car. Zack handed her the phone and Chloe stuffed it in her pocket before following the three men to the rear of the car. Skid opened the trunk. Her eyes bulged when she saw the wide array of guns.

Everyone looked at her.

"You're going to tell me to stay in the car, aren't you?"

Zack stared at her for one long moment. Finally, she shrugged and headed to the backseat.

"If you come," he said. "You've got to do exactly what I say when I say it. Have you ever fired a gun?"

She shook her head. He handed her a small dark handgun. "Here's the safety. Flip it. Like this." He demonstrated. Over his shoulder, she could see the Cube shaking his head.

"Chloe, pay attention. Squeeze the trigger, here. It has a kick. So expect it. Promise me you won't fire unless it's absolute necessary."

She nodded, swallowing hard. The men were busy assembling firearms and packing their pockets with innocent looking items.

Staying in the car was looking good.

Chapter Twenty Nine

Chloe stood outside the car holding the gun in her hand for a full three minutes while the men armed themselves. The heavy, cold pistol gave her the creeps. Could she fire it? At a person? Could she live with herself if she killed someone? How much bad karma would that bring her? Or worse how many years of therapy would it take for her to recover if she actually pulled the trigger? What if she closed her eyes when she fired and killed one of the SEALs by mistake?

Zack reached for the trunk lid.

"Take it back. I won't be able to fire the gun. All I'll be doing is providing a weapon for someone who probably doesn't need one."

"You're sure?"

"Positive."

He returned the gun to the trunk. "Good call, Nancy Drew." His approving gaze encouraged her. She'd done the right thing.

"Would you feel comfortable carrying a knife?"

She thought about it. A knife wouldn't necessarily kill someone. "Yeah, I could handle a knife."

Zack ignored the wicked looking blade strapped to his leg and handed her a switchblade from his pocket. It was heavier than she expected. The metal case was engraved with a diamond pattern, making it rough to the touch. Chloe found stroking it with her thumb surprisingly soothing.

His large hands covered hers and his warmth seeped through her skin. "Place your thumb against this stud and push."

The blade snapped open. Its jagged edge looked sharp and dangerous. Forget Nancy Drew. Lara Croft could kick ass.

"How do I close it?"

He showed her. She practiced several times until it seemed effortless.

"When you're a Jet, you're a Jet all the way…" she made a few jabbing motions as she sang under her breath, forgetting that the microphone picked up every sound.

"Chloe…" Zack spoke softly into her ear.

"Sorry," she mumbled.

"You ready?"

At her nod he showed her some basic hand signals. "Stay behind me."

Chloe followed Zack as closely as she could. The knit cap itched. Her sandals weren't made for hiking. And the heavy knife reminded this could turn ugly in a heartbeat. But she's wouldn't have turned around for all the money in the world. She rubbed the grooved surface of the knife like a worry stone, hoping it would take away some of the tension.

They headed north at a parallel line to the warehouse. About a block and a half later he turned east. "We're covering the rear," his voice whispered in her ear as they traveled beyond the warehouse.

His deep voice carried no further than the mic. She doubted she would have heard him if they'd been standing next to each other. No wonder he ran ten miles a day. She panted like a race horse with the exertion of keeping up.

"Do I need to slow down?"

Rats. She'd forgotten he could hear her and

would be paying attention. They were probably all thinking bringing her was a big mistake. She wasn't over weight, just out of shape. She pressed her lips firmly together and inhaled through her nose.

"I'm fine." She clenched her thumb and middle finger together in an acupressure technique to give her more stamina. His pace slowed. Whether it was for her benefit or not, she couldn't tell, but she didn't complain.

Three large oaks separated the narrow parking lot and warehouse from the fence. Zack stationed her behind the trees. A strong chemical scent wafted through the air. Ammonia. Nothing but the warehouse was close enough to emit such strong odors.

Zack's voice, almost a soundless whisper, spoke to her. "You can see from here. The tree will shield you. Don't come any closer unless I call."

Chloe nodded, searching the area carefully. With the exception of the trees, shelter from gun fire was almost non-existent. The paved parking lot circling the large metal warehouse was deserted. The vehicles she'd seen earlier were obscured from her view.

He worked his way closer to the building.

"I'm in," a toneless whisper in her ear said. Zack stood in front of her. Either the Cube or Skid had managed to get inside.

"Seven men dismantling the place. A truck and a suburban inside. Equipment going into the suburban and the truck is getting the chemicals and trash. An eighth man coming from the back."

Chloe recognized Cube's voice as he spoke. How had he gotten inside the building without being seen? Doors were at the front and the back. The only windows were at the very top of the building, largely designed to give light.

Chloe's cell phone rang. Quickly she grabbed it, but she heard a distinctive "shit" in her ear.

She pulled the headset off to answer the phone. The caller was Glyn. "I can't talk now," Chloe whispered into the phone. Glyn refused to be put off.

"Where's Zack?"

"Busy," Chloe murmured. A man she didn't recognize stepped out the rear door and Chloe slid behind the tree and dropped to the ground in the hopes the meager shrubbery would help hide her. Cautiously she peeked around the tree. Zack was nowhere to be seen. The man paced to the edge of the building, looked up and down the empty parking lot and then went back inside.

"Glyn? You still here?" Chloe turned so that her back was to the tree. That way her voice even which she kept it at a low whisper would carry away from the building.

"Yes. What're you doing?"

"Never mind that. Tell me what Stanley does for a living."

"He's a chemist for OHSA. He investigates biological hazards. Why?"

Oh, my God.

"I'll call you back." Chloe disconnected the call and turned the phone off.

"You stupid little fool." Stanley snarled standing above her, holding a much bigger gun than the one she'd held. For a man she'd always considered a nerd, he managed to look menacing enough now.

"Get up." He grabbed her arm, jerking her to her feet. With the other hand he pulled the cap off her hair and flung it to the ground. Then whirled her around so she faced the building. His heavy flannel shirt scratched her neck as his arm tightened and forced her back against his chest. He pressed hard against her windpipe and cut off her air while the cold metal gun barrel bore into her temple.

"Where are your friends?" He ignored her frantic noises for air.

Her instinct was to fight, but instead she forced herself to still, hoping Stanley would think he'd subdued her. No one saw what was happening. She went limp against his body and he eased her arm.

She gasped for air, trying to suck as much down into her lungs as possible.

"It's just me," she wheezed out.

"Liar."

Think. "I followed you from the grocery store. You acted so weird I was worried."

Stanley paused. Chloe prayed he bought her excuse, but she couldn't see his face and feared turning her head. Her headset was somewhere on the ground, but Chloe refused to look down and alert him to the nature of her lie.

"I don't believe you."

"It's true. What're you doing here?"

"Getting rid of some problems. Apparently, more than one." He pushed her out from behind the tree and shoved her forward. Another man exited the rear door. Stanley took the gun away from her temple momentarily to gesture him back inside.

Chloe jammed her hands in her pocket. Her fingers curled around the knife. The knife wasn't soundless when it opened. There was a loud click when it snapped into place so she had to be ready to use it.

She shifted it to her left hand where Stanley

couldn't see it. Then realized the knife was designed for right-handed use.

Sweat beaded on her forehead and between her breasts. Surely she could do this. Was there a movement in an upper window?

Now or never. Her body tensed and she stopped walking catching Stanley off guard. She bent double making a retching sound. Her stomach lurched as she opened the knife. Puking was a very real possibility. By the time he'd pulled her to him tighter, the knife was open and in her left hand.

She wished she could practice her stabbing motion, but there was no time. She jabbed upward and felt the blade skim over the sleeve of his heavy shirt and travel further piercing her own ear.

Blood spewed everywhere. Chloe squealed more in shock than pain.

Stanley jerked back, but before Chloe could run, he grabbed her hair and pulled her tight to him. A shot struck the ground at their feet flinging bits of pavement upward.

"I'll kill her," Stanley yelled, pressing the gun against her temple.

Warm liquid dripped down her chest. The smell of blood revolted her. She fought the lightheaded, woozy feeling. The sticky blood splattered her face. Trickles dribbled toward her chin.

Stanley's arm tightened at her neck, forcing her to measure her breathing in shallow quick breaths.

"Pritchard. Show yourself. Tell your men to back off." Stanley yelled in her ear.

Automatically she strained away from his voice, but he held her firm. "You move again and I'll kill you just for the fun of it." The effeminate overtones she'd always associated with him had disappeared.

No matter what else happened his plan included killing her. If she died, she'd never be a PhD. Would the world be worse off with one less PhD? Her life wasn't important. The fight drain out of her. Breathing didn't matter.

Nothing mattered.

Zack stepped around the corner of the building, his hands in the air. A large machine gun with a hollow stock pointed toward the sky. He was giving up?

"Let her go."

How could he appear so calm? It was one thing for her to die, but Zack couldn't give up. His mission was important. Life was never fair, but it would be the height of irony for him to die at the hands of Stanley, a worthless nothing. And worse it would be her fault.

He couldn't die.

"Gun down. Now." Stanley yelled in her ear.

Chloe wanted to close her eyes but she couldn't stop looking at Zack, who didn't move, except to say, "Let her go."

"I'll blow her away now." Stanley banged her temple with the edge of the barrel. The smell of putrid fear filled her nostrils. He was terrified. Chloe wasn't afraid of death. Everybody died. If she could save Zack in the process then she wouldn't have died in vain.

"Before she hits the ground, you'll be dead. It isn't worth it, Stanley. Let her go."

Fuzzy thoughts filled her head, but not before she heard Stanley growl. The lack of clean air swamped her. She refused to give in to weakness.

Zack never looked at her, but his eyes burned a hole in Stanley's face. With a diversion he could get a clean shot. She'd forgotten about the knife that she still held in her hand. She stroked the handle. She shifted it to her right hand and turned the blade. She couldn't miss again. Silently she chanted affirmations for strength and courage.

My body is a temple. It has no flaws.
I am being guided by the light.
What is supposed to happen, will.

Her hips swung out as her arm sailed backward with as much force as she could master. The razor sharp blade hit true. She pushed it home as his arm loosened, she dropped to the ground. Stanley's wail filled the air. Shots rang out. He exploded above her and crumpled on top of her.

Chloe lay completely still, afraid to call attention to herself. She couldn't see. She couldn't move. The smell of blood was everywhere. Sticky, oozing liquid seeping in her clothes. She bit her lips to keep from puking. Her heartbeat pounded in her ears.

Any moment the men inside the warehouse would blast outward to investigate the noise and an all-out gun battle would erupt.

Stay safe, Zack.

She trembled under Stanley's weight.

# # #

Zack covered the thirty feet between them faster than he'd ever run. He'd never felt so paralyzed in his entire life as he had watched her standing before him, blood spreading across her shirt, her complexion pasty white and dirtied with splatters of blood while Stanley held the Glock to her head.

His team had subdued the men inside. Zack could take Stanley any day, any time, but he couldn't risk Chloe. She gave him the time and the opportunity he needed. If she was dead, everything had been for nothing. He needed her. He loved her. Living without her would be impossible.

"Chloe," he shoved Stanley's body aside and gathered her into his arms. Blood pooled on the ground. Her clothes were covered. An HK had some fire power and he hoped this was Stanley's blood and not hers.

"Chloe. Talk to me."

She moaned. Her arms circled around his neck and clung. He crushed her to him.

"A-man get an ambulance out here and find Thompson Michaels."

"I'm ahead of you. The ambulance is on the way. How's she doing?"

"Don't know," he answered. "Where are you hurt?"

"I stabbed myself," she wailed. Zack almost cried with relief that she could speak.

"What? Where?" he demanded. His hand soaked with blood from her body.

"My ear, I think." She turned her head to show him where she'd stabbed herself,

"Are you hurt any place else?"

"I don't think so, but yuck, I hate all this blood." She twisted her head to look at Stanley. But Zack held her firm. "Don't look." He wanted to cry, to laugh. Hell, to sing. She was all right. The worst thing that had happened was that she'd nicked her ear. He chuckled.

"Are you laughing?"

"No," he assured her, examining the minor cut.

He held this thumb and finger to her ear to slow the bleeding. "I'm happy. But I'm never letting you near another weapon. You're a dangerous woman."

"If I hadn't thought he was going to kill you, I wouldn't have stabbed him again."

"You stabbed him to save me?" he asked barely able to believe her convoluted thinking. "It wasn't me he was holding a gun on."

"The SEALs need you. America needs you."

"Let's clean you up and get you home." He lifted her in his arms and carried her toward the front of the building.

"I can walk."

Stanley's men lay bound on the ground. "Put me down. I look like a fool." She whispered to Zack who set her on her feet. Seven men lay face down on the hard concrete.

"You captured all these men and I didn't hear a thing. Amazing."

The Cube grinned. She studied the men on the ground.

"Bubba," she squealed, sounding as girlish as possible. "It's good to see you again."

Bubba raised his head and squinted his eyes at her. Recognition flittered across his face. Chloe crouched. "You're going to find out sooner or later, anyway. But I should tell you. I was Gordy's girlfriend, you lying, murdering bastard. You're going to go to jail for a million years. And I'm going to be one of people who put you there."

Sirens screamed nearby. "Let's get you away from here." Zack said, offering an arm to pull her up. "Michaels will be pissed we interfered as it is."

Skid pulled up in the car. Zack opened the trunk and found a couple of t-shirt and shorts. "Hide in the bushes if you want, but put these on." He pulled his blood soaked shirt over his head and tugged on another cleaner black t-shirt.

Chloe eyed the sparse woods and opened the car doors to create privacy. She stripped and redressed as quickly as possible before collapsing into the backseat, grateful that the leather seats could be cleaned if she got blood on them.

Thirty minutes later, Detective Michaels stuck his head in the car. "You okay?"

She forced herself to sit upright. "I'm just glad it's over."

"Yeah, me too. I'll check on you next week to see how you're holding up."

Chloe nodded unable to speak. She knew what he meant. He'd check on her after Zack left. The events of the afternoon paraded through her mind. She thought with a clarity that had been missing until now.

Zack would leave, but she'd survive. When push came to shove, she could do what needed to be done. She was strong. Able to stand on her own. She loved Zack but she had to let him go. Indiana lay ahead of her. A new beginning. Her life beckoned. She sat up, feeling better than she had in months.

Watch out world. Chloe La Ruse is coming your way.

Chapter Thirty

"You coming with us?" Cube asked Zack as he and Skid opened the car doors.

"No, Michaels and I are going to talk to Glynnis. Take Chloe home. Pack our stuff. I'll be a couple of hours."

He stuck his head in the back window to check on Chloe. "Sure you don't want to go to the hospital?"

"Yeah. I'm sure."

# # #

As Glynnis slumped further into the chair, Zack put his arm around her for support. She'd listened to the detective tell her Stanley was dead.

"What you're saying is impossible. Stanley was incapable of such guile. He was in the choir at church. He took care of his parents. He did NOT manufacture meth in his spare time."

"John Wayne Gacy was a clown and worked with kids," Thompson pointed out. "People can surprise you with their secret lives."

"Nothing you can say will convince me he was involved. Have you been following him? How did you know about this anyway?"

Zack outlined almost everything they'd done. He skipped mentioning the tracking device he'd put on the detective's car since Thompson was sitting beside him and probably wouldn't see the humor in it.

"I still don't believe it," she said.

"Glyn, he was a chemist. He rented a warehouse in his own name. And when Chloe alerted him to trouble, we caught him in the midst of breaking it down. Plus he held a gun to Chloe's head and was prepared to kill her. How much proof do you need?"

She looked so despondent Zack tugged her tighter to him. "If what you say is true, why didn't I know it?"

"Stanley was a master of deception." Detective Michaels said. "Many criminals are able to blend into society and hide their true identities."

"You did know it on some level, Glyn. You didn't marry him," Zack whispered into his sister's ear.

Glyn harrumphed, but quit arguing. She pressed her lips together reminding Zack of their mother. "I'm so glad to be leaving this town. You'll come with me to tell mother?"

He agreed. His mother would be harder to persuade than Glyn. When had he become the quixotic man of the hour? Thompson left them at Glyn's little red Miata. She slid behind the driver's seat as Zack climbed into the front. His knees were bent double as he squeezed into the tiny seat.

For a woman who had two brothers who loved to drive, Glyn paid no attention at all. She cut other drivers off and turned across traffic without enough space. The thought of a turn signal was unknown to her. He'd never been so glad to be stopped as when she pulled into their mother's driveway. "There's no reason for you not to stay at the house tonight. All the guests have left."

"I'm not staying. You and mother will be upset, but Chloe had a gun held to her head today. She needs my support more."

Four hours later, Zack wondered how many times he would have to repeat that statement. Bernice's over the top reaction to the news had Glyn insisting they drive her to the hospital for a sedative. This time Zack insisted upon driving their mother's car. At the hospital Glyn left them in the waiting room and disappeared into the bowels of the building.

His mother sat still for the first time since she'd heard the news. The disarray of her appearance testified to her emotional state. Her hair, normally so tidy, stuck out in wiry clumps combined with her un-tucked blouse and her disheveled skirt, she resembled a homeless person.

But her breathing had returned to normal.

"I was so sure Arnie's level-headedness would rub off on his children. And yet, you're the only one who remains calm during a crises. Who would have guessed it?"

Zack wasn't sure if she was thinking out loud or actually speaking to him.

"Arnie was a strong influence on me as well," he said hesitant of the reception of his words.

Bernice's lips curled in a dreamy smile. "He was a good man." She nestled back in the chair. "Arnie never felt you weren't his son just because he wasn't your biological father. I miss him."

"Me, too."

"Would you think less of me if I signed up for some counseling?" she asked, sounding surprisingly insecure.

Zack shook his head. "No. In fact after this week, we could all use it. Maybe we can get a family discount."

Bernice leaned her head against his shoulder, and Zack draped an arm around her. They sat together in comfortable silence for several minutes.

Finally, Bernice said, "Let's find Glynnis and go home. I'm feeling better."

# # #

Chloe soaked in a hot tub. The bloodstained pink tint in the water disturbed her enough she closed her eyes and then showered to rid herself of any residue before she got out.

Wrapped in her warmest chenille robe she lay in bed listening to the low murmur of the men's voices in the living room. When they called her to join them for dinner, Zack still wasn't back.

The living room no longer looked like command central, if one discounted the white board and flip chart against the far wall. "Have you packed Zack's clothes yet?" she asked, sitting down at the table.

"No. We're leaving tonight. He's staying another day or so."

The men worked hard to entertain her during dinner telling her humorous stories of their childhoods rather than SEAL tales of danger. The A-man and the Cube had been high school buddies. A brother of the A-man headed up another team. They regarded themselves as the three musketeers.

"If they are the three musketeers, where does that leave you?" she asked Skid.

All three spoke at once. "D'artagnan." Chloe laughed, but didn't tell any stories of her own.

Toward the end of the meal, Cube checked his watch and nodded at the other two.

Skid cleared his throat and rested his elbows on the table. "We took a vote and made you an honorary SEAL team nine member. You won't get a plaque and nobody will ever know you did anything but us."

The A-man rocked back in the wooden chair taking the front two legs off the ground. The pride in his voice had her blinking back tears. "You followed the code of the SEALs by being loyal to the team. You served with honor and integrity. You were ready to lead, ready to follow and you never quit."

The Cube finished by saying, "Most importantly, you fought to win."

Chloe struggled not to cry. She couldn't accept this award and shook her head to refuse. "I could never do what you do. I couldn't put myself on the line every day. I've known Zack for eight years, but I never understood what he did until this trip. He was always special, but I never knew how much."

The three men were quiet as Skid filled each of their wine glasses and raised them in a toast. "Nancy Drew, we think you're special, too."

Chloe laughed unable to control her emotions and when tears trickled down her cheeks the men laughed as well.

All three rose. "We hate to eat and run, but we've got a plane to catch," Cube said.

"Sorry about leaving you the dishes," the A-man added.

"You cooked. I'm willing to clean." She waved from the door even after they were in the car and backing away from her building.

Before doing the dishes, she dismantled her crime scene flip chart and white board and stored them in the second bedroom. Today had been a nightmare. The close skirmish with death including the blood, the gore, and the fear had been horrific. Feeling her knife pierce a man's flesh was revolting. The thought still made her ill.

But…

The excitement of being put in extreme danger had exhilarated her. Her blood had raced and she'd never felt more alive in her life. Being a teacher was safe, but it wasn't the same as feeling each pore vibrating with life.

As she finished the dishes, she eyed the couch longingly, but didn't sit. She still had one more chore left to finish. The one she dreaded most.

Chapter Thirty One

Zack climbed the stairs to the apartment and grinned when the door opened. She'd been waiting for him. He was glad his men had left, so they could have some time alone. A couple of nights at least. Then he'd head out and she'd go to graduate school. Maybe he'd visit her.

But when her blue eyes met his, they held no joy. His heart twisted seeing her unhappy.

"How are you feeling?"

"Okay."

He stepped into the living room and took a quick inventory. Gone was any evidence of his team or Chloe's investigation. The only thing out of place was Zack's packed bag, which sat in the middle of the coffee table. "I still have some leave coming. I was going to stay here a couple more days."

Chloe made a low humming noise in her throat and looked at the floor. She picked at the chipped polish on her fingernails. "Tonight would be better."

He couldn't believe it. She was asking him to leave? "Why?"

"It's time to move on." Her voice was firm even if she was determined not to look at him.

His vision went red, he grit his teeth, refusing to give in to his need to yell. "I see. What if I don't agree?"

"So we could have sex one more time?" Her calm voice was like a knife in his heart.

"There's more to it than that." What did she think? He didn't care? He loved her.

"No, there's not."

She might as well have run him over with a truck. She didn't love him. SHE DIDN"T LOVE HIM. Even repeating it didn't lessen the impact. Hoisting his duffle he flung it over his shoulder. What could he say to make her take it back? Nothing came to him.

"At least let me pay you for all the groceries you bought."

"No." She opened the door wider than it had been.

Zack stepped toward her. It was over. He couldn't just walk away. How could he leave without kissing her one more time?

In the doorway he put his finger under her chin and raised her face. She closed her eyes but her tear soaked cheeks and lashes told the true story. Saying goodbye was killing her, too.

Much as he hated it, he recognized the truth of her position. There was nothing he could offer her. He was a SEAL. SEALs always left. She was just a pretty young girl, the one who'd stolen his heart.

Gently, he kissed her lips one last time and stepped out into the warm night air. Nothing remained here for him. The safety of Riggers had been a dream. Nothing more.

He sat behind the wheel of the rental car for a long time. What did he want?

He wanted to walk back up the stairs and make love to her one more time. He wanted to tell he loved her. He wanted to promise her he'd never leave. For the first time he wanted something more than he wanted to be a SEAL.

Chapter Thirty Two

Three weeks later as Chloe packed her belonging into boxes, a loud pounding on her door made her jump.

Her heart raced. Who could it be besides Zack? She peeked through the peephole. Detective Thompson Michaels stood on the other side. Taking a deep breath she opened the door.

"Did you check before you opened the door?" He pointed at the peephole as soon as the door swung open. "I could be anybody."

"You sounded like a SWAT team."

He laughed. "Just keeping you on your toes."

She stepped back to let him enter.

His stature, the quick scan of the apartment, the loose Hawaiian shirt that almost covered the bulge of his shoulder hoister all reminded of his profession. "You moving?" Partially filled boxes covered the floor.

She tugged the blue bandanna from her head and shook her hair free. His eyes followed the movement of her breasts making her self-conscious. The raggedy cutoffs and old t-shirt, perfect for cleaning and packing, were less charming to entertain company.

Inviting him inside suggested trouble. Thompson Michaels was only one notch removed from being the predator Zack was. Chloe remained in the small entrance to talk. She wasn't nervous, but found herself clutching the doorknob.

"Indiana University. PhD. I leave in three weeks."

Was he here for a reason? He certainly appeared

casual as he leaned against the door jam.

Unlike Zack, the Detective was not a slave to blue jeans in his off hours. He wore khakis and an incongruous Hawaiian shirt that somehow he managed to make work despite the bright peacock blue and sunshine yellow splashes of color. Even without the jacket, gun and badge, he still radiated a cop persona with his close clipped hair and square jaw. But it was his knowing eyes that made the flesh on her arms pebble.

"And then what?"

"Well…" She expected her answer to surprise him. "Believe it or not. I've been talking to the FBI. They're encouraging me to take a lot of languages and call them when I'm done."

"I'm amazed. The FBI?" He crossed his legs at the ankles. "What does Zack think about this?"

Chloe glanced out the door at the bright blue Texas sky and the scattering of soft cottony clouds. She was ready to leave, but she'd miss Texas with its wide-open spaces and endless blue sky.

"We ended on a rough note. I doubt I'll hear from him."

Thompson made an almost imperceptible noise in his throat reclaiming her attention. A feral look of elevated interest crossed his face.

No way were they going there.

"Don't even think about it," she cautioned. "Didn't you mention a girlfriend the first time I met you? Or are you thinking of a ménage?"

His look shifted to amusement as he raised a questioning eyebrow and crossed his arms on his chest. "You'd be up for that?"

"No."

"Too bad," he said. "I see a woman now and

then, but if that bothers you I could end it."

Great! Just what she needed. Another man who radiated intensity when she was the flavor of the month, but could turn disinterested in a heartbeat. "I've already had one fling this year. I'm not looking for another."

Thompson straightened. His height dwarfed her. Chloe shifted on the balls of her feet before taking a step backwards.

He must have read the concern in her face, because he didn't press his advantage. "I'd make a great rebound boyfriend." He grinned, though Chloe suspected his smile was a feign to the left, like smiling would make him less dangerous.

She shook her head. "You're a nice guy, you deserve better than that."

"Really I don't," He assured her, still persisting in the amused, harmless angle.

Chloe didn't smile.

"Just dinner between crime-fighting friends?"

"No." She refused to prolong the conversation and waved toward the door in a way to indicate it was time for him to leave. "Thanks for dropping by."

He hesitated as though searching for another avenue to pursue. Instead, he reached into his pocket and said, "My card. Call if you get lonely."

Chloe accepted the card and watched him walk down the stairs to the parking lot. Her fist curled crumpling his number into a tight wad.

"You are not the answer to my loneliness," she said softly as she closed the door and tossed the card into the trash.

Five minutes later another knock caused her to

look up from her reading. Was the man refusing to take no for an answer? Begrudgingly she went to the door a second time. But her caller wasn't the Detective.

This time she opened the door to a young, vaguely familiar woman who held a chest in her arms.

"Sylvia Arnold," she said, identifying herself. A smile crossed her features. "My husband and I bought your grandmother's house."

"Of course," Chloe said grateful to place her. "Won't you come in?"

"Just for a moment."

Sylvia stepped into the entrance, but unlike Thompson, she kept walking into the living room. As Chloe closed the door, Sylvia placed the chest on the coffee table.

"The air conditioning went out this week," She turned to face Chloe. "The repair man found this chest behind the furnace. I don't know how long it's been there. We opened it hoping for some treasure."

Sylvia laughed. Chloe moved closer to view the chest.

"Unfortunately for us, it was filled with your grandmother's papers. We started to throw them away, but decided you might want to go through them."

"I do. Thanks for bringing it by. Do you like the house?"

"We love the house. We're making the charming little attic room into a nursery."

Chloe nodded. "I grew up in that room. I hope your child adores it as much as I did."

Sylvia let herself out. Chloe plopped down on the couch to sort through the papers. Why would Gram keep a chest of papers behind the furnace?

The chest contained the warranty for the toaster and the sales receipt on the Pinto. In 1972, Gramps had paid two thousand, one hundred twenty-nine dollars for a car that ran well for almost forty years. He'd gotten his money's worth. Despite what others thought, she snorted in a defensive way, it had been a classic when she had driven it.

There were more papers but most of them meant nothing. Either they were for appliances that had long since been discarded or were newspaper articles about people Chloe didn't know.

A few church bulletins had made it to the mix. She was sorry to admit the contents of the chest were mainly junk. So why had her grandmother hidden it? None of those papers was particularly important.

The chest had a dome lid and was made with heavy dark green canvas and wood slats like a smaller version of an old actor's trunk. If she painted the canvas yellow and the wood white, the chest would look nice as a little planter.

Not too much could be done with the lid. The arched shape was attractive from the outside but solid on the inside. Chloe opened the chest several times. The lid was heavier than the chest. The last time she peered inside a sliver of white wedged in the corner of the lid that hadn't been there a minute ago. Chloe ran a fingernail around the edge of the lid. It moved.

She pried harder. The lid popped open leaving the interior of the dome exposed. Or it would have if the photographs, envelopes and a telegram hadn't been crammed into the tiny space.

The girl in the collection of photographs could only be one person - Paula Marie La Ruse - Chloe's

mother. Paula Marie looked like a blonde version of
Gram. Chloe poured over each picture. Most were
school photos. Her mother had been a cheerleader and
a Camp Fire Girl. The very last picture in the stack
was a very pregnant Paula holding a bouquet of white
roses gazing up at a tall blond man. Chloe turned the
photograph over. On the back in her grandmother's
spidery handwriting was the notation, Paula and
Doug, Wedding, May Second.

Chloe's birthday was May twenty-ninth. Her
father's name was Doug. Chloe's birth certificate was
no secret. There was no father listed despite the fact
her parents had been married.

Her grandparents never spoke about her mother.
Why? What was the big secret? Why had they let
Chloe think she was illegitimate when she wasn't?

Chloe studied the envelopes of both the letter and
the telegram. Both were from Quito, Ecuador. A
telegram would not be good news. A second envelope
was address to Clarence, Chloe's grandfather. Chloe
recognized her grandmother's writing, but couldn't
imagine why that letter would be hidden also.

She exhaled, blowing out all the air from her
lungs. Then inhaled deeply. Heat flooded her cheeks
and she fanned her face with the South American
letter before opening it.

Dear Mom and Dad,
Who would have ever dreamed we would be
in Ecuador with the Peace Corp? Sargent
Shriver, Peace Corp founder came personally to
the plane to see us off. Quito is known as the
middle of the world, being only fifteen miles
south of the equator. You'd think it'd be hotter
than Texas, but because it's in the mountains,

the weather remains fairly cool.

We are scheduled to leave for a village community near the Colombian border in the morning, but tonight we celebrate our vision. I know you and dad disapprove of my being here, particularly since I had to leave Chloe behind. I couldn't deny Doug his dream just because I got pregnant. Nor could I let him come alone.

Chloe will be safe with you. It is only for two years. We will return and become a happy family with many more children. I'll think of you constantly and promise to keep detailed notes in my journal. I plan to read them to my daughter when she's older so that she will know the importance of putting into action one's beliefs.

XOXOXO, Paula

Chloe sat back stunned. Of all the things she had imagined her mother's life to be. This was not it at all. Why would Gram hide this information?

The telegram was the bad news that Chloe expected it to be. Her parents had never left Quito, but had been killed in a local insurrection only hours after the letter had been mailed. The incident, the official telegram stated, was under investigation.

Chloe studied the envelope with her grandfather's name on the outside. It remained sealed. Never opened. Obviously never read by him.

Her hands trembled, but she managed to get a finger underneath a corner and ripped a strip large enough to remove the solitary piece of paper. Her grandfather was dead. While it seemed like a violation of his privacy, there was nothing he could do about it. But her heart pounded and she licked her lips to moisten them. The handwritten note from her grandmother read:

My dearest love,

If you are reading this you have discovered the secrets I have kept from you all these years. Our daughter whom you loved so dearly did marry before Chloe was born. I convinced her to keep it a secret because I knew you would be crushed that she elected to be married by a Justice of the Peace and not include us.

I believed that when they returned from South America we could have another wedding and do it right even though Chloe would have been a toddler by then.

They died so unexpectedly, I selfishly kept the knowledge from you. Because it would have broken your heart and spirit. I needed your strength to go on and raise our wonderful granddaughter, our daughter's last gift *to us.*

I always planned to tell you, but after a while so much time passed that even I began to believe Paula would one day walk through our front door again with Doug at her side. We would laugh and all hurts would be forgotten. Now I realize that only in Heaven will that happen. I regret my decision to hide this from you and hope you will one day forgive me.

Love, Mary Alice

Every decision her grandmother made had been out of love, but the ramifications of her actions had caused far deeper hurts. Chloe stretched out on the couch. Her parents were dead, but she hadn't been abandoned. They had loved her. She needed to share this information with someone.

Zack. He was the only one who would care. Why had she pushed him out the door? Why hadn't she told him she loved him? Why hadn't he loved her back?

She punched the buttons for Zack's number on her phone. A recording devise answered. "I can't come to the phone. Leave a message."

Short, brusque, but hearing his voice again made her tears fall harder. It wasn't the loneliness that got to her. It was the fact Zack wasn't here. She could go on. She knew that. He'd shown her that. But what good was life without love?

She called his line fifteen times that evening and listened to his words. It was immature and childish. Had he ever answered she would have been too embarrassed to talk. But it was a long night and somehow hearing his voice made it appear like he cared.

The next day, she slept late. It was mid-morning when she finally dragged herself off the couch and stumbled to the kitchen. Pulling open the telephone directory, she dialed the local number for telephone service. After being assured that her call was really important no less than twelve times, she finally reached a live person.

"How may I help you?"

"I need to have my phone disconnected."

"Are you moving? Can we set up new service in another location?"

"No. I'm leaving. I'll never be back."

Chapter Thirty Three

"Demon!"

Zack glanced over his shoulder to see Commander Mittleton's head poking out of his office.

"Sir."

"Got a minute?"

He pivoted on his heels and retraced his steps. The Commander closed the door. Both stood in the tiny office hardly big enough for the desk and two chairs. The glass floor-to-ceiling windows were designed to create the illusion of spaciousness. The men were equally matched for size and brawn. Their closeness sucked all the air out of the room.

"Congratulations are in order."

Zack kept his face impassive as he awaited the news. The Commander handed him a letter. "The promotion came through."

He genuinely tried to look pleased about it, but somewhere in the back of his mind he could hear the death knell ring.

"I know what you're thinking," Commander Mittleton said. "But we don't just need men in the field. We need experienced warriors to direct the operations and train the newbies."

Zack nodded. "I know."

"Good." The Commander appeared satisfied.

"I just don't think it's me."

"Think it over, carefully. Your leadership would be an asset."

"I will."

The Commander was nobody's fool. He didn't press but stepped aside to allow Zack to exit. This discussion would be continued later. Although to his way of thinking there was nothing left to discuss. Wasn't life special?

Earlier that afternoon, he'd refused to meet Cube and the team at the Rusty Nail for drinks. After the strenuous week of training exercises, he'd pleaded exhaustion and paperwork. He wasn't exhausted. He knew it. His team knew it. But he was sure as hell having a hard time getting back into the swing of things since returning from his sister's non-marriage only a few weeks ago. Calling himself every kind of fool, he turned the steering wheel and drove his car toward the popular Rusty Nail hangout.

Honky-tonk music blared into the parking lot. Needing the distraction of beer and friendly company he entered and headed toward the bar.

"Demon," a voice he recognized yelled above the music from the juke box.

Most of his crew was clustered around a couple of tables pulled together. He snagged a waitress, ordered his beer and tossed her a five. "Keep the change."

"Thought you weren't coming," Cube said as Zack slid onto the chair next to him.

"Changed my mind." The waitress put the beer in front of him. Skid snatched a short stack of photographs from the table and put them in his lap.

"What are those?"

"Nothing."

He raised an eyebrow. Skid took a long swallow of his drink. "Nothing?" Zack repeated when Skid finally took his glass away from his lips.

No one at the table spoke. Zack searched the various faces and found discomfort or embarrassment on the few he could see. Most of the men found distractions that caused them to turn their heads.

"Oh, show them to him," A-man said, disgust filled his voice. "He doesn't care anyway."

Cube cleared his throat and shifted his chair further back. Skid slapped the photos down and headed for the bar. A couple of others followed him. Zack took a long swallow of his beer before stretching across the table to pick up the four-by-six photos.

Chloe. In her cap and gown. Boxes stacked in the spare bedroom. Working at the computer. Several of a classroom. One with her standing in front teaching. Another of her laughing. If he looked closely he could probably count her molars. It wasn't a beauty shot and yet it looked so like her. The photos smacked him hard.

He raised his eyes from the pictures. "Where'd you get these?"

Austin, the A-man answered, "I sent her a digital camera for her birthday and she sent these photos."

"Her birthday?" Another blow. She'd had a birthday?

"Oh, man. What's wrong with you? There were eight thousand Gemini horoscopes posted all over that apartment. It wasn't a stretch to figure out she had a birthday coming up."

"She had a digital camera," Zack protested.

"Rinky-dink." A-man snorted. "I sent her a camera that she'll be able to use at the FBI. Plus Skid and Cube sent her the tripod and a high quality photo printer."

"The FBI?" What the hell did the FBI have to do with it? Zack searched the younger man's face.

"Uh… yeah. You didn't know?" A-man drummed his fingers on the table. "This is your fault. Why the hell did you break up with her?"

He rose to his feet and leaned across the table. "WE ARE NOT GIRLFRIENDS. My personal life doesn't involve you."

"You called us to Texas, why?" A-man demanded.

Zack slammed his beer on the table and headed toward the door.

"Demon," Cube called, running to catch up with him.

"What?"

"The only one who doesn't know how you feel is Chloe. You need to go after her."

He grunted and stepped out into California sunshine. *Go after her. Like that would solve all his problems.*

# # #

Chloe stood at the white board. "In our last class before the final I'd like to talk about something other than the anatomy and physiology of sex. I'd like to talk about love. This isn't going to be on the final so I don't care if you don't take notes."

Most of the students laid their pens down and looked expectant. "Love as you know takes many forms, but I want to discuss romantic love. How many of your grandparents stayed married?"

Hands shot up.

"Wow. A lot," Chloe said. "How about your parents?" Fewer hands waved. "I'm sure all of you have friends who thought they were in love, maybe even married and one day they broke up or announced they were getting a divorce."

Several heads bobbed.

"Some of those couples surprised us. We thought they were happy. And some, we wondered why it took so long for them to break up." Several people laughed.

Chloe pressed on. "My question is this. What makes love stay?"

Several students picked up their pens again. Chloe laughed. "If you're expecting I have the answers to the secrets to the Universe, you're going to be disappointed. I'm asking you. In your experience why do some people fall in love and stay in love and others don't?"

"Compatibility," a girl on the front row said.

"Humor," another female student suggested.

"Money," a guy near the back hollered.

"No doubt that's why you never hear of any celebrities getting divorced," Chloe said dryly.

The class laughed.

"I have a theory," a familiar voice spoke from the far side of the classroom. Chloe's head pivoted to watch Zack rise from a squatting position hidden behind a row of students. What was he doing here? Why hadn't she seen him come in?

She racked her brain to think of something clever to say, but her mind could only focus on how good he looked. He crossed his arms across his chest in his superman pose and Chloe's throat went dry. The man lacked real style in his wardrobe choices. But the one outfit he owned in duplicate, he made work. Chloe would never look at plain black t-shirts and jeans the same way ever again.

He tilted his head. "Would you like to hear my theory?"

Oh, yeah.

"Certainly," she replied pleased with how professional she sounded. If only she had some water. She wet her lips and swallowed to relieve her parched throat.

A faint shadow of a smile crossed his lips. He probably knew exactly how she felt. Hell, she was acting like a middle school girl with her first crush. She stepped closer to his side of the room to hear every word he spoke.

"We expect love to be everything, to take care of us, to never let us down and most importantly to allow us to live happily ever after." He shook his head sadly. "But if love were easy it'd have no value. To make love stay, you have to want it more than anything else in the world. And here's the secret... You have to work at it. Every day."

"Sometimes that's not possible," Chloe said, shifting from one foot to the other. She clasped her hands behind her back to still them and keep her jerky movements at a minimum. "What if one person's obligations make it impossible to commit?"

"Then love isn't a high enough a priority for them."

"What if there are too many obstacles in the way? Like living in different areas of the country or needing to finish school or having a demanding job?"

"Well, some of those problems might be overcome if both people sat down and were honest about how they felt and each was prepared to compromise."

"You came up with this theory on your own?"

"I had help. Some of my teammates shared some ideas."

Something about the way he said that made her

suspect his teammates had volunteered their thoughts unsolicited. "What ideas?"

"Could we discuss this without an audience?"

Chloe looked around. The room was filled with students spellbound by the interplay between Zack and herself.

"Class dismissed," Chloe said and waved her hand to make the students disappear.

Her magic waned, because the freshmen filed out of the classroom more slowly than they'd ever moved before. Several of the girls in the front row purposely lingered. It occurred to Chloe that she and Zack would never have privacy on campus.

"My apartment," she said. "Fifteen minutes."

Zack grinned. "See you there."

Chapter Thirty Four

With each step Chloe took toward her apartment, she attempted to bolster her defenses against Zack and her road-weary heart. What was he doing here? Why was he talking about love? Did he think that she would give up her dreams just because he uttered the three words, "I love you?" Was that why her mother was able to go to South America even when she had a baby?

Chloe loved Zack. She knew it. He obviously knew it, too. But when he talked about compromise did he mean she should give up school and move to California to be by his side? Was that what true love meant? The female had to do the compromising?

He couldn't give up being a SEAL. That was as ingrained in him as his DNA. And she wouldn't want that anyway.

A block from her apartment a large rental truck parked by the curb. It wasn't actually the truck she noticed first or even the trailer attached to the hitch. But sitting on the trailer was one of the hottest cars she'd ever seen. She had no idea what model of car it was, but even without test driving, Chloe bet this silver beauty went a hundred miles an hour standing still.

Eight years with Gordy made her appreciate a fast, well-designed sports car. He would have loved this car.

Gordy and his dreams.

How miserable he'd been because he couldn't make them happen. If only he'd gotten on with NASCAR, none of this would have happened.

Gordy would be at some racetrack. Zack would

be in California. Glynnis would be married to Stanley. And Chloe would be in Indiana becoming a sex therapist.

What was she saying?

This all happened for a reason. It was karma that Glynnis hadn't married Stanley. And Chloe found out she wanted more excitement in her life than teaching. She'd have never investigated the FBI on her own.

Now she needed languages. That could happen at any major college in the nation. She didn't have to go to Indiana. She could live in California.

"Do you like it?" Zack asked, coming up behind her. Chloe jumped. "Sorry, I didn't mean to startle you."

"Do I like what?"

He tilted his head and gestured toward the car. "Who wouldn't?"

His eyes glistened with pride. Chloe's head swiveled like a spectator at a tennis match. Car. Zack. Car.

"Yours?" she asked finally making the connection. She should've known that cars would matter as much to him as to Gordy. He nodded.

"I can hardly wait to drive it." She teased him, knowing the Pritchard men would never let someone else touch their precious machines.

Zack dug into his pocket and handed her a set of keys. "You're going to love the way it handles."

"I am? You'd let me drive it?"

"That's what your set of keys would be for. Of course, you could use them to scratch your name into the paint, but that lowers the resale value."

"My keys?"

He nodded toward her hand in case she'd forgotten she was holding them. "The ones in your hand."

"Are you giving me the car?"

"I thought we'd share it. Eventually we'll want a second car."

"You'd trust me drive it?"

"Honey, this is a piece of metal. It's a well-put together piece of metal, but it's still a thing. I'm trusting you with something much more valuable."

She shook her head, trying to overcome the feeling of floating in space. "You are?"

His smile deepened. His deep brown eyes sparkled in the sunlight. "Yeah. My heart."

He opened the truck door and reached inside. A bouquet of white orchids in a perfect green glass vase appeared in his hand. "I brought you flowers." He handed her the vase.

Chloe dropped her backpack to the ground to clutch the vase to her chest and inhale deeply.

"Orchids. They're gorgeous. These must have cost a fortune."

"I thought roses, but, according to the Internet, Gemini's don't like roses."

"Who says?"

"Some astrological chart."

"Some astrologer who has an orchid business on the side. Surely you don't believe all that hooey about horoscopes?"

"No. But you do. You read your horoscope every day."

"Yeah, but I don't live my life by it. I make my own decisions. And frankly I like most flowers including roses but violets are my favorite because they remind of my grandmother." Chloe laughed.

"But maybe I'll shift to orchids, because they remind of you."

He grinned. "If you choose stinkweeds, I could give you flowers every day of the week."

"Only on the nights we're eating head cheese for dinner."

"It promises to be a fragrant relationship."

He leaned over to pick up her backpack. Wrapping an arm around her waist, they walked toward her apartment. He trusted her with his heart. Chloe clutched the flowers to her chest so tightly she feared it might shatter. He came back for her.

"Why do you have a moving truck here?" The truck didn't fit into the picture.

"I quit the Navy."

Chloe quit walking. "WHAT? How could you do that? You love being a SEAL." She searched his face for answers, but Zack only shrugged.

"My job was changing and I love you more than I wanted to make changes."

"What? Are we?… I'm not… Do you?… Is there?…" Chloe sputtered.

"Breathe," Zack commanded. "I have a job lined up in Indiana."

Chloe's mind refused to contemplate what he'd said. "You do?"

"Driving Indy cars. It'll be great."

"You're coming to Indiana? To be with me?"

Zack stopped smiling. He placed a finger under her chin and looked her in the eyes. "Is that okay?"

"Sure… fine… perfectly okay." *Could she sound any stoopidier?*

"But I want to get married here."

Chloe nodded in agreement when his words finally sunk in. "To me? Your family hates me."

"They'll come around. And look at the high point. My mother won't want to plan our wedding."

Neither would she. What'd she know about weddings? Tentatively, she asked. "Do you have some ideas?"

"Uh huh. Parking lot of J Nors. Instead of smashing cake in each other's faces, we'll throw beer."

Chloe laughed. The tension left her. Zack wanted to marry her. He loved her. Karma for once was working out. Not that she would choose to throw beer at her wedding.

"Maybe I'll plan our wedding," she suggested in self-defense.

"You do that. I wanted to buy a ring, but the astrological guide said no diamonds. They recommended a pink tourmaline."

Chloe rolled her eyes. "Promise me you'll throw that guide away."

They resumed walking toward her apartment. Life was going to be great. They were following their destiny. This wasn't a dream where she'd wake up lonelier than before.

"I'm a Scorpio, by the way," he said as they started up the stairs to her apartment.

"Like I couldn't figure that out. The sex sign of the zodiac," Chloe snorted and held out her left hand imagining a diamond ring already on it. "I think your diamond will look great on my hand."

"Well, it'll have to be a big one, because I want the world to know you belong to me."

Chloe looked at her finger again imagining an even larger stone. Beside her she heard Zack chuckle.

"Will you teach me how to drive an Indy car?"

"Sure."

"And pick locks and scale tall buildings."

"Maybe," he said, caution had entered his voice.

"Maybe?"

"I would only teach those things to a woman who loved me."

"I love you."

He cupped a hand to his ear. "What? I didn't hear you."

"I LOVE YOU."

Sadly, he shook his head. "I think you're going to need to tell me a few more times."

"How many?"

"At least every day for the next fifty years or so."

Chloe grinned. "I can do that, but just remember paybacks are hell. And furthermore, I have a serious question for you."

"What?"

"Just how many black t-shirts do you own?"

"We can count later. Right now, I can think of other things to do."

THANK YOU!

Thanks for reading The Wrong Brother, the first book in the Wrong Series where Wrong Never Felt So Right. I truly hoped you enjoyed it.

If you liked this book, tell a friend, write a review, or send an email. If you hated this book, tell me why. Let me know where I have failed to value your time. I welcome any comments you would like to make.

If you would like to be notified of the next book in this series. Please go to my website at: www.Nancybrophy.com and sign up for my newsletter. Or you can email me at: Nancybrophy@gmail.com. I appreciate hearing from readers.

Made in the USA
Middletown, DE
11 June 2022